RL 3.8
pts 1.0

# A TALE OF THE UNDERGROUND RAILROAD

# FREEDOM SONGS

by Trina Robbins
illustrated by Jason Millet

**Librarian Reviewer**
Laurie K. Holland
Media Specialist (National Board Certified), Edina, MN
MA in Elementary Education, Minnesota State University, Mankato

**Reading Consultant**
Elizabeth Stedem
Educator/Consultant, Colorado Springs, CO
MA in Elementary Education, University of Denver, CO

STONE ARCH BOOKS
Minneapolis   San Diego

Graphic Flash is published by Stone Arch Books
151 Good Counsel Drive, P.O. Box 669
Mankato, Minnesota 56002
*www.stonearchbooks.com*

*Library of Congress Cataloging-in-Publication Data*
Robbins, Trina.
    Freedom Songs: A Tale of the Underground Railroad / by Trina Robbins;
illustrated by Jason Millet.
    p. cm. — (Graphic Flash)
    ISBN 978-1-4342-0445-5 (library binding)
    ISBN 978-1-4342-0495-0 (paperback)
    1. Graphic novels. I. Millet, Jason. II. Title.
PN6727.R56F74 2008
741.5'973—dc22                                               2007032233

Summary: Fourteen-year-old Sarah is a slave in Maryland during the 1850s. She
knows her only chance at freedom is to the North, where slavery is illegal. To get
there, though, Sarah needs help from members of the Underground Railroad. But
who can she trust? The road to the promised land will not be easy.

Art Director: Heather Kindseth
Graphic Designer: Brann Garvey

1 2 3 4 5 6 13 12 11 10 09 08

Printed in the United States of America in Stevens Point, Wisconsin

072009
005594R

# TABLE OF CONTENTS

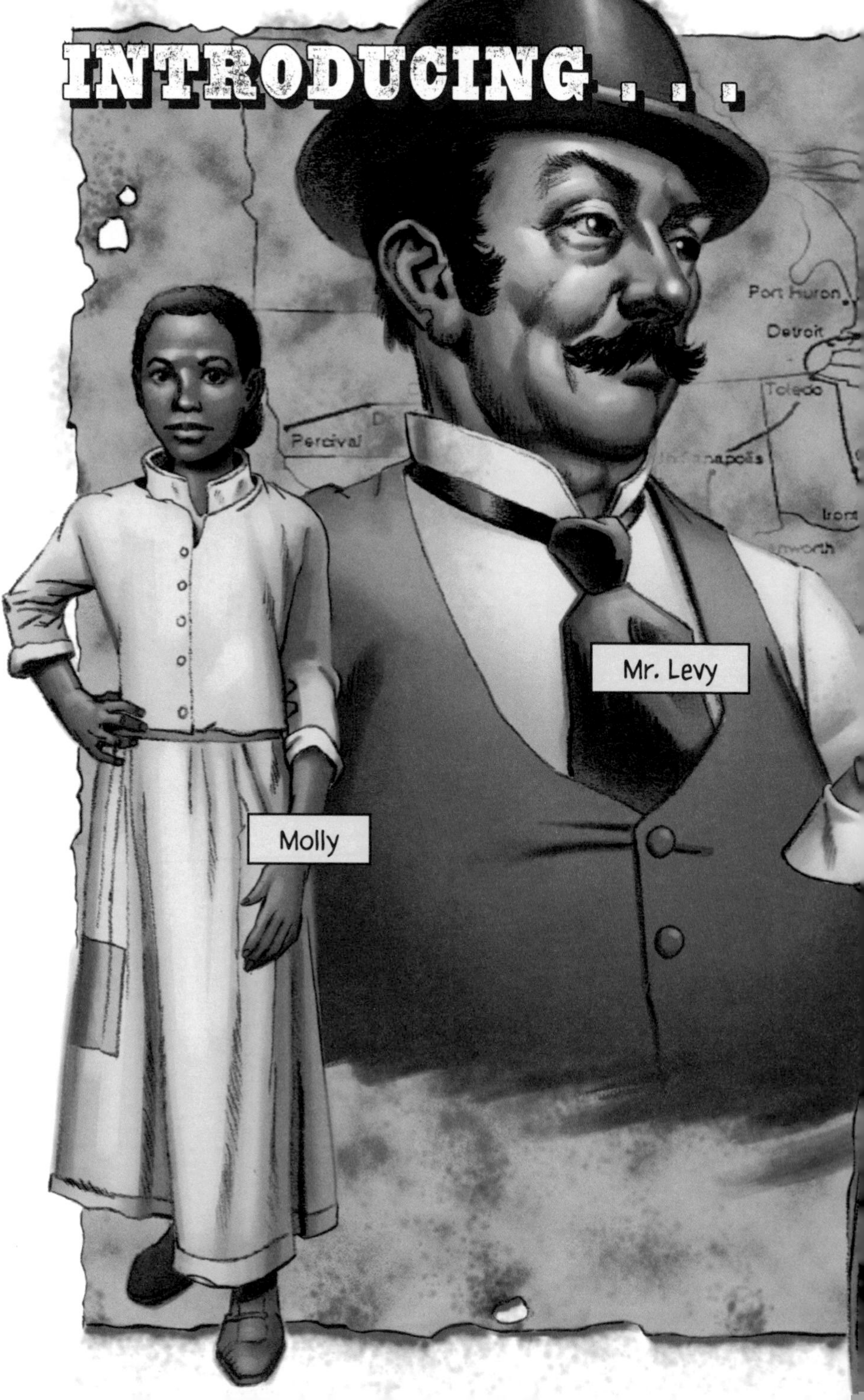
INTRODUCING . . .
Molly
Mr. Levy
Percival
Port Huron
Detroit
Toledo

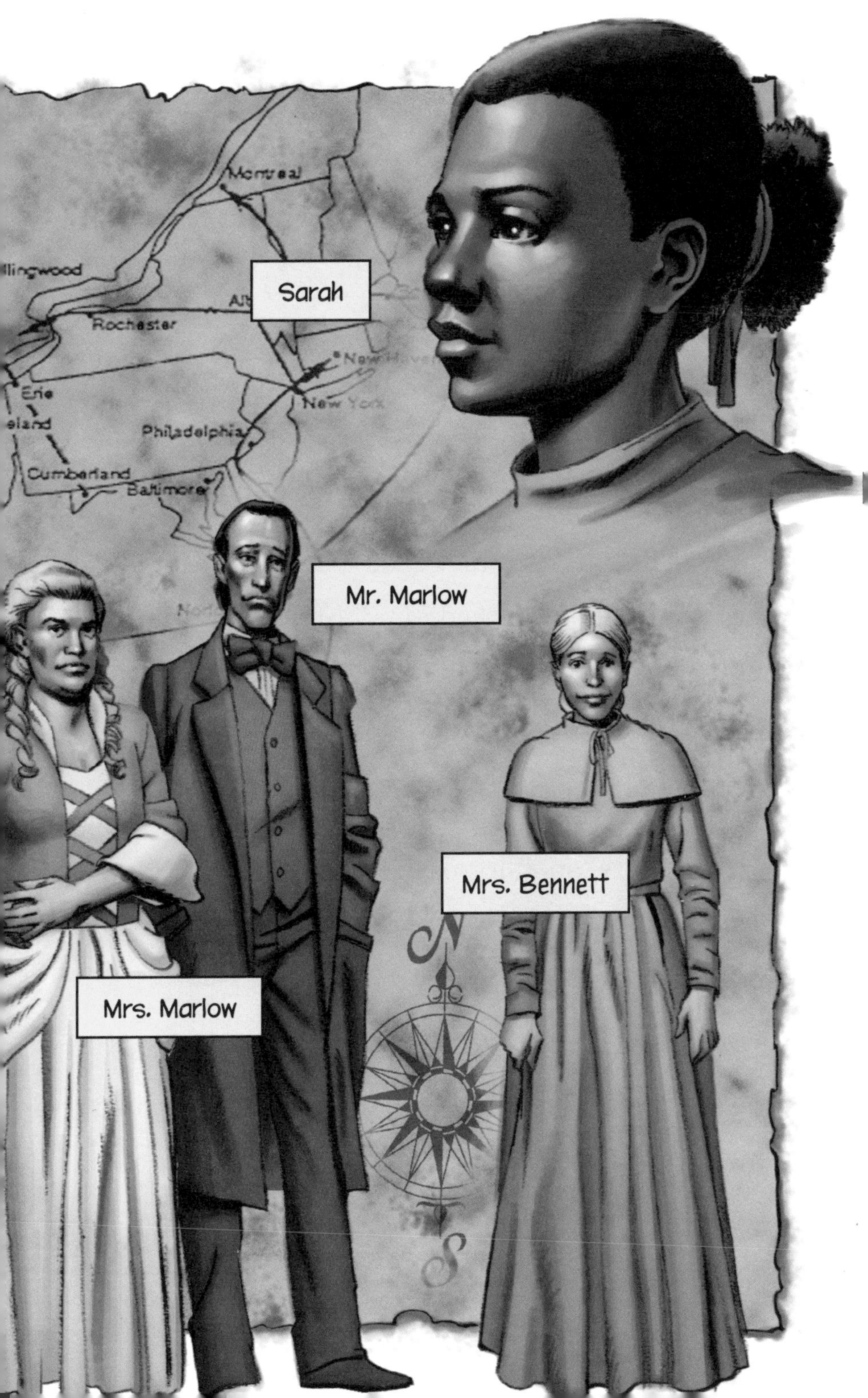
Montreal
llingwood
Rochester
New York
Erie
Philadelphia
Cumberland
Baltimore
Sarah
Mr. Marlow
Mrs. Bennett
Mrs. Marlow

# CHAPTER 1
# OH, FREEDOM!

Smack!

A hard slap woke me from a dream about my momma's pancakes drenched with sweet maple syrup. The slap knocked me right out of my chair. I had been sitting up all night, fanning flies away from Mrs. Marlow's baby.

I guess I fell asleep.

"You lazy, good-for-nothing girl!" Mrs. Marlow screamed. "My poor baby has fly bites all over her face!"

I couldn't talk back to Mrs. Marlow. She was my mistress. I had to obey her because she owned me. I was a slave, and she could do whatever she wanted with me.

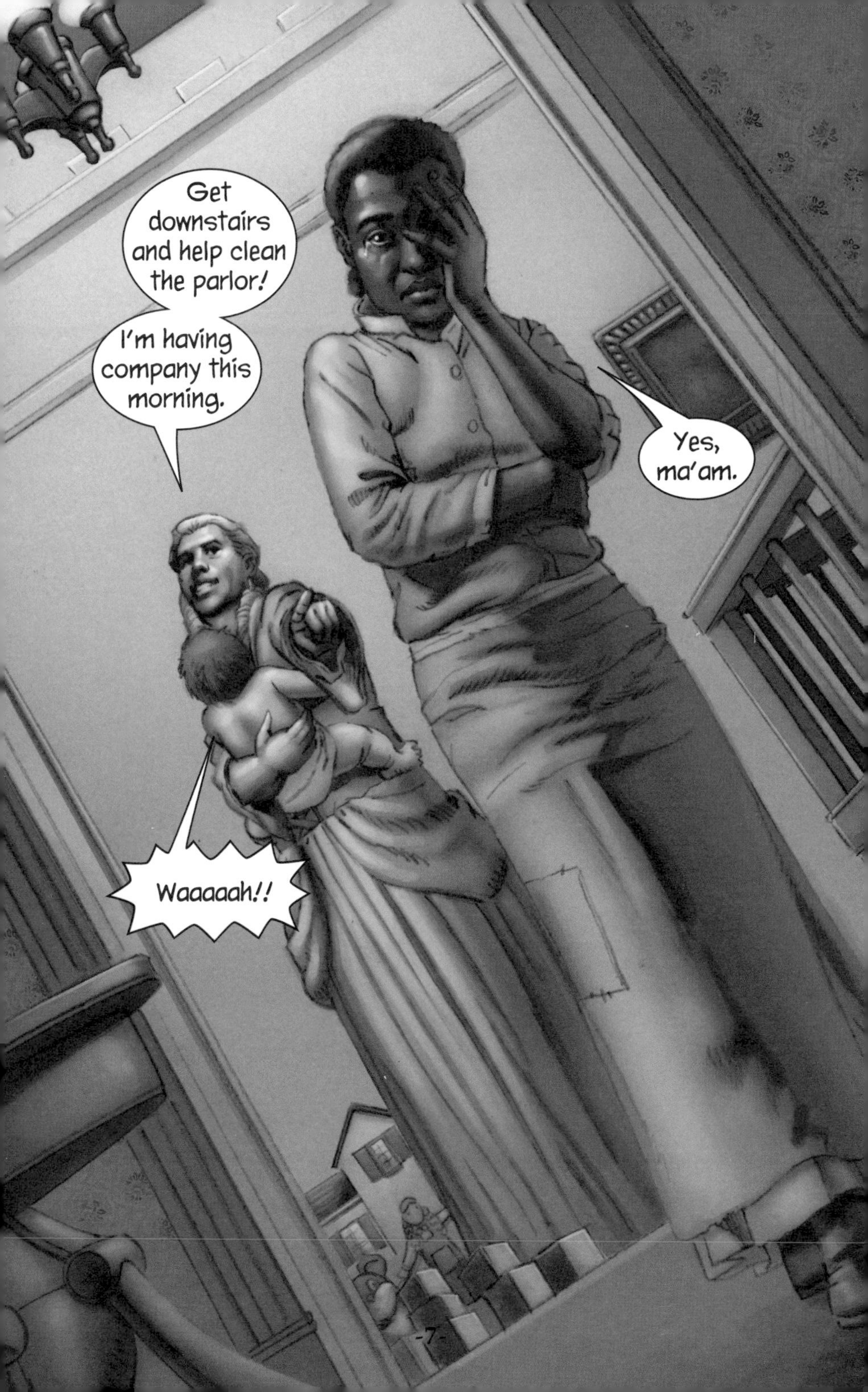
Get downstairs and help clean the parlor!
I'm having company this morning.
Yes, ma'am.
Waaaaah!!

Mrs. Marlow was so mad that she didn't let me stop for breakfast. I had to go straight to the parlor and make up the fire. Then I served lemonade and fresh-baked cakes to the guest.

Mrs. Marlow's visitor was a traveling peddler, Elijah Levy. She always liked to see him when he came by. He brought beautiful silks and laces for her to make into dresses. He entertained her with stories about all the places he traveled. It seemed like he had been everywhere in the world — or at least in America.

"I just came back from Philadelphia," said Mr. Levy. "Folks there don't agree with slavery, but the women sure do like pretty silks."

As I filled the glasses with more lemonade, Mr. Levy glanced at me. I could tell he was looking at my red and swollen cheek. He knew my mistress had slapped me. I felt so ashamed.

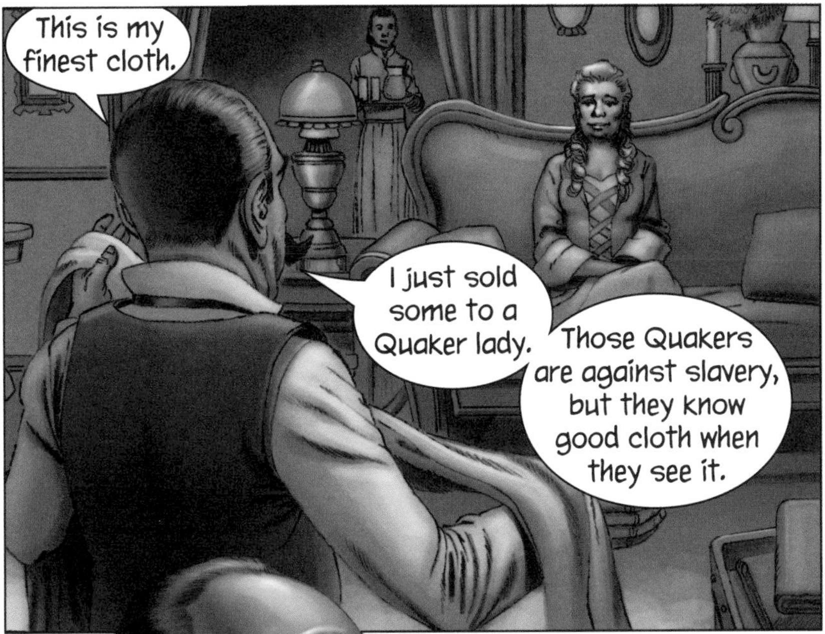
This is my finest cloth.
I just sold some to a Quaker lady.
Those Quakers are against slavery, but they know good cloth when they see it.

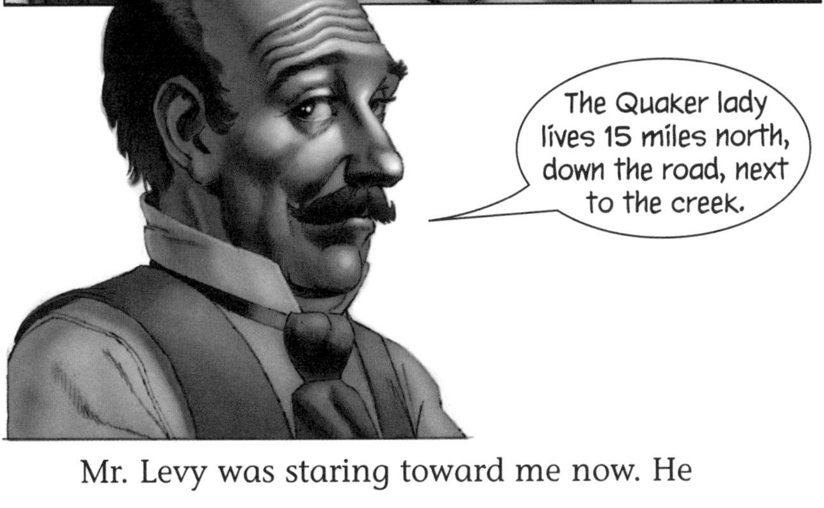
The Quaker lady lives 15 miles north, down the road, next to the creek.

Mr. Levy was staring toward me now. He was aiming those words at me! But what was he trying to say? I only had a moment to think before I heard Mrs. Marlow yelling again.

"These cakes are burned! Take them back to the kitchen, and throw them away," she shouted.

"Yes, ma'am," I replied softly.

The cakes didn't look burned to me. They smelled awfully good, too. I hadn't eaten all day, and I was starving.

As I put the tray down on the kitchen table, I thought about taking just a small bite. I knew Mrs. Marlow would punish me for even a nibble. But it sure was a waste to throw away good food when I was so hungry.

I looked to make sure no one was watching.

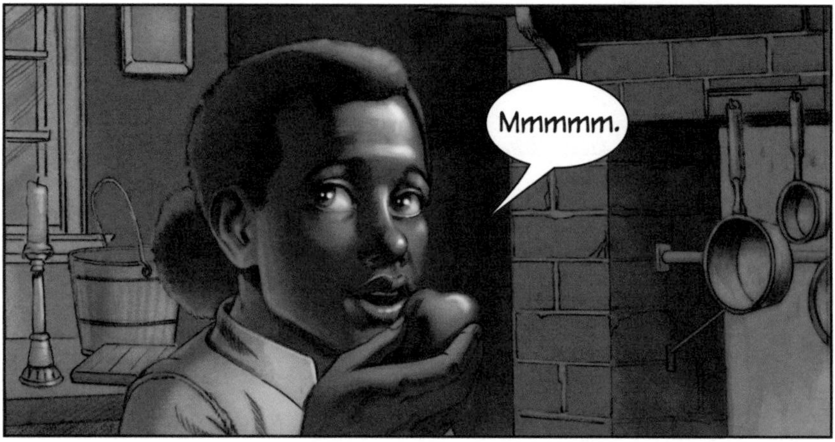
Mmmmm.

They were delicious! Slaves never got to eat anything as fine as cake. We just considered ourselves lucky to get enough food to survive.

Then, just as I was going to swallow my first bite, I heard footsteps behind me.

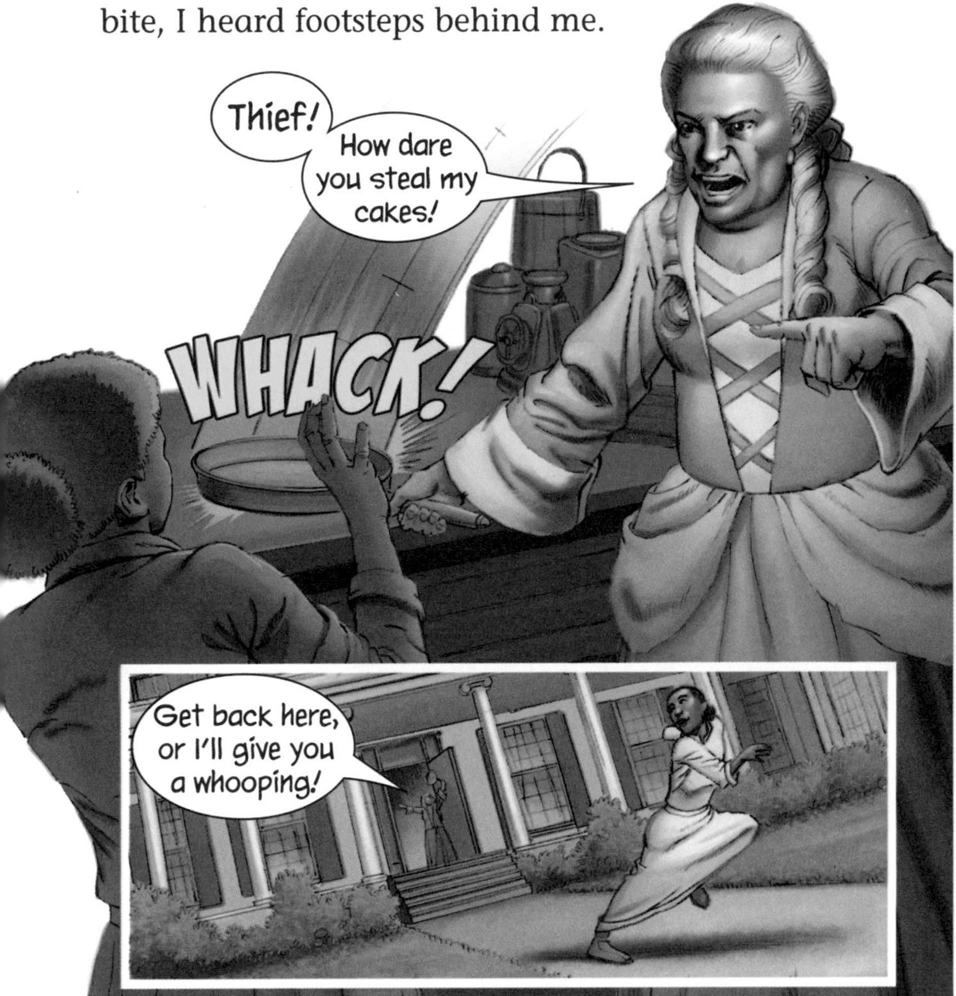
Thief!
How dare you steal my cakes!
WHACK!
Get back here, or I'll give you a whooping!

As I ran from the house, I heard Mrs. Marlow tell the cooks to give the cakes to the hogs. Even though they had fallen on the floor, I would have given anything for another bite.

Mrs. Marlow was sure mad at me! I tried to stay away from the big house all day, but I could hear her through the open window. She was complaining about me to my master, Mr. Marlow.

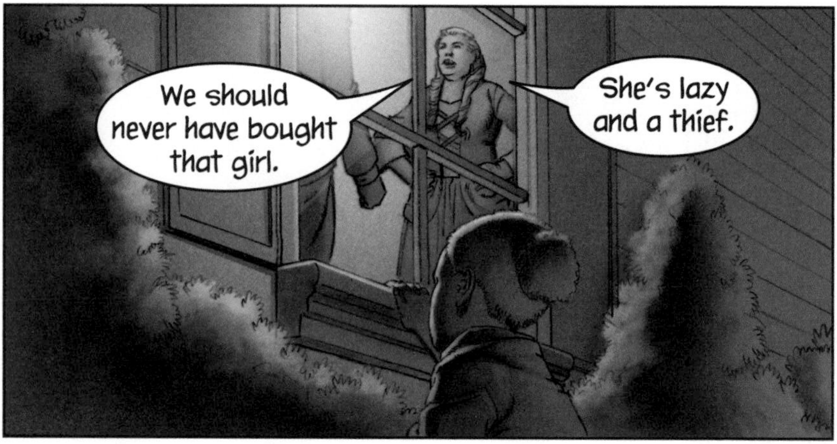
We should never have bought that girl.
She's lazy and a thief.

It wasn't fair! She'd seem lazy, too, if she had to stay up all night. I knew Mr. Marlow was going to punish me. I thought he would make me work in the fields. I wasn't prepared for what he said.

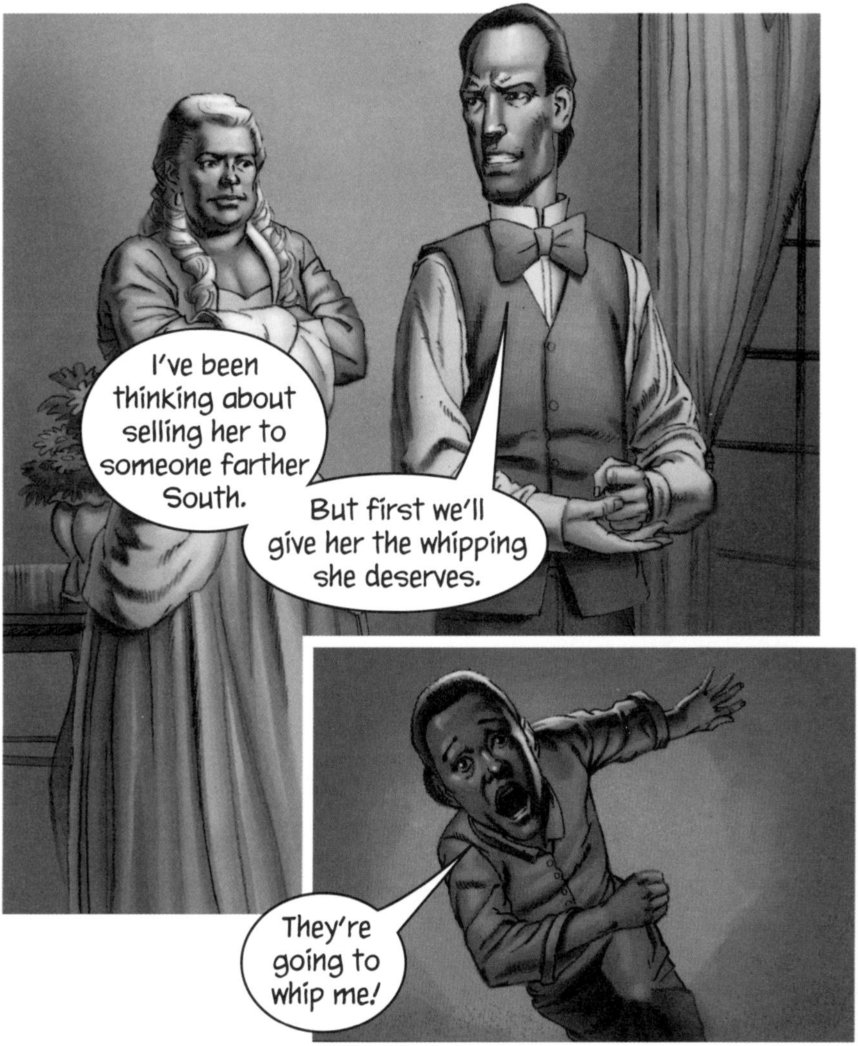
I've been thinking about selling her to someone farther South.
But first we'll give her the whipping she deserves.
They're going to whip me!

I had never been whipped, though my mistress sure had hit me enough times. But I remember when my master whipped a field hand just for being too slow. It was horrible! The poor man's back was covered with blood afterward.

I wouldn't let them whip me. I wouldn't let them sell me farther South, where slaves were treated even worse than here in Maryland. I had to run away! I had to take that risk!

I waited until nighttime. That way, I wouldn't be missed until the next morning.

I couldn't leave without saying good-bye to my mother. She was owned by another family, and she lived a mile down the road. When I was ten years old, they had sold me to the Marlows. We were property, and our masters could sell us just like they would sell a horse or a cow.

I cried when I was first separated from my mother, but at least I could walk down the road and visit her. Now I would have to leave for good.

As I approached the house where she lived, tears filled my eyes. She was washing dishes, and I tapped on the window to get her attention.

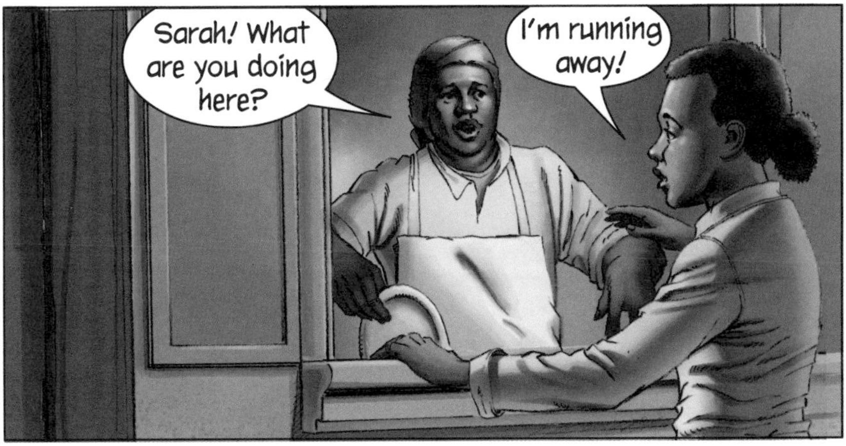
Sarah! What are you doing here?
I'm running away!

I told Momma everything. She understood but started to cry. It broke my heart to see her so sad.

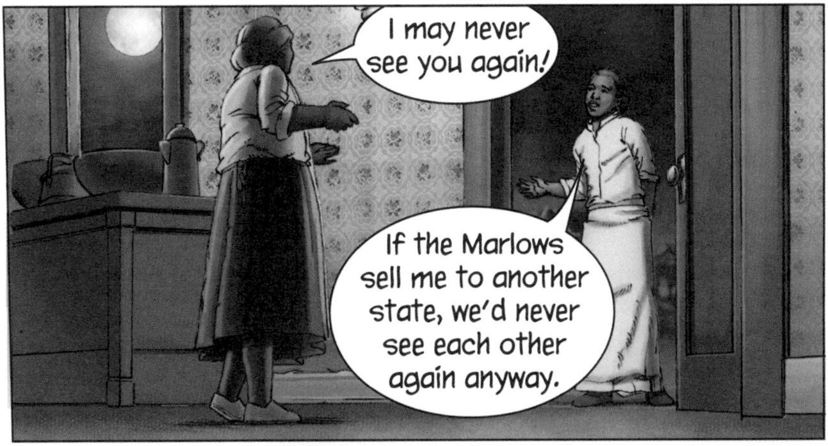
I may never see you again!
If the Marlows sell me to another state, we'd never see each other again anyway.

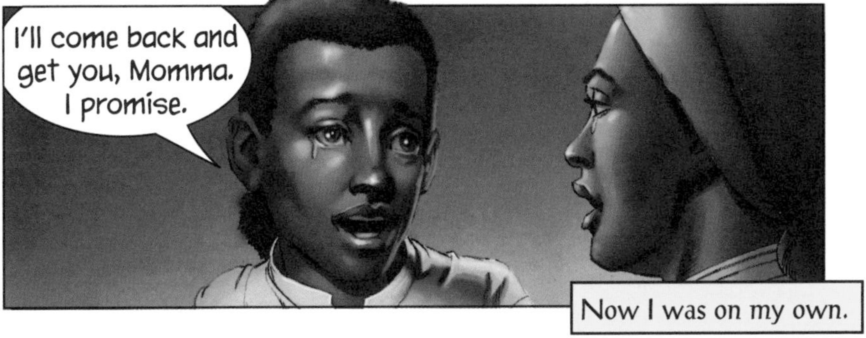
I'll come back and get you, Momma. I promise.
Now I was on my own.

# CHAPTER 2
# FOLLOW THE DRINKING GOURD

The peddler said that a Quaker lady lived 15 miles north. I didn't know much about Quakers, but he said that they were against slavery. Maybe she would give me shelter for the night.

I knew the way north. I looked for the pattern of stars in the sky that some folks call the Big Dipper and others call the Drinking Gourd. Slaves sang about the Drinking Gourd because those stars point north. In the Northern states, slaves were free. The white folks don't know that the song teaches us how to escape.

As I traveled along the moonlit trail, I had to be careful. When the master found out I was gone, he would send the slave hunters after me.

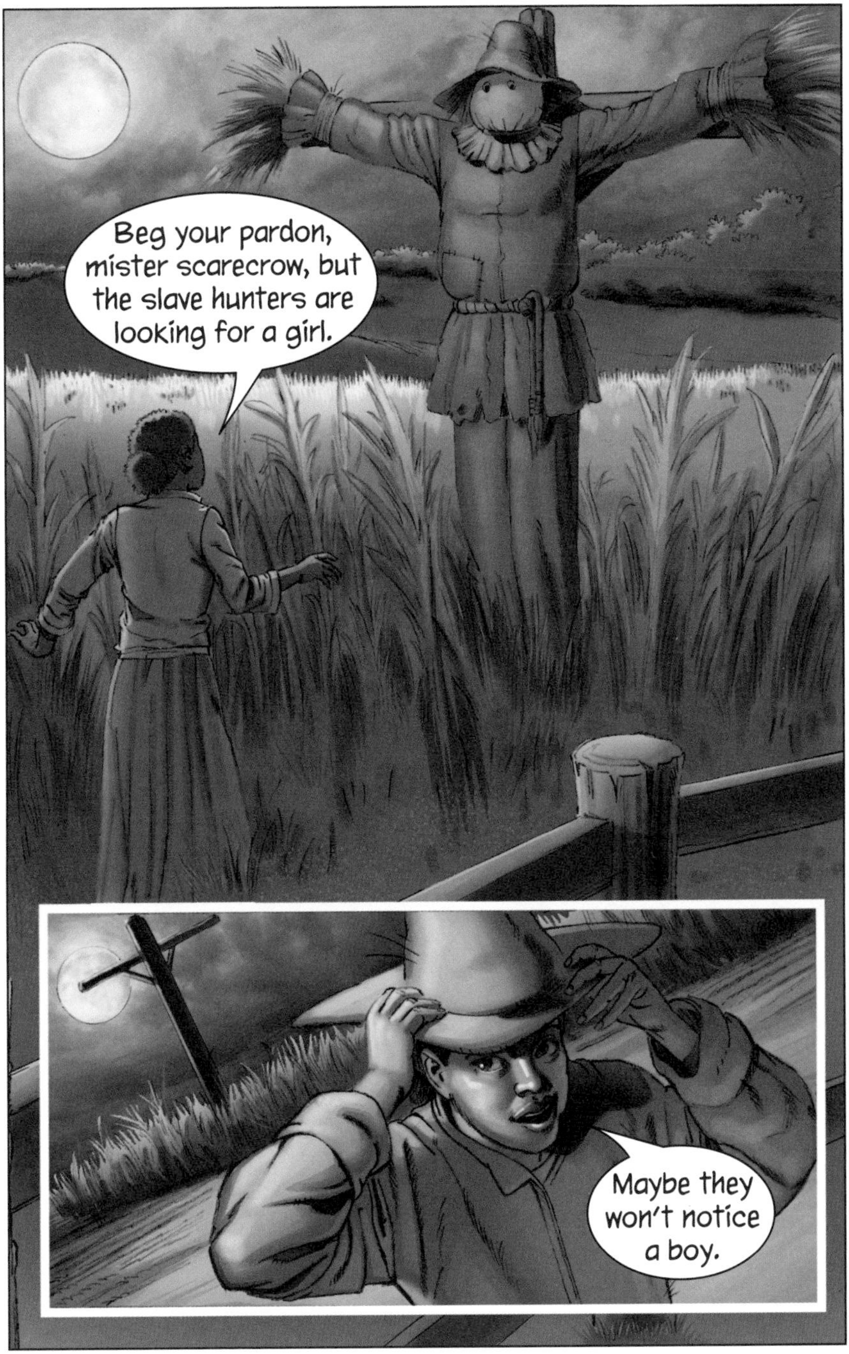
Beg your pardon, mister scarecrow, but the slave hunters are looking for a girl.
Maybe they won't notice a boy.

It was almost morning by the time I got to the Quaker lady's house. The moon had left the sky and gone back to sleep. I wished I could sleep, too. Fifteen miles is a long way to walk, and I hadn't slept much the night before. I hadn't eaten anything either, except for a small bite of cake.

I started to knock on the door, then stopped. What if this was the wrong house? What if the peddler had lied? Maybe there was no Quaker lady! Or if there was, what if she turned me away, or worse, brought me back to the Marlows.

I decided that waiting until morning would be safer. Maybe then I could see if the house really belonged to a Quaker lady.

For now, the barn next to the house looked like a good place to rest. I went inside and fell onto a stack of hay, piled in an empty horse stable. The hay was soft and warm, and I quickly drifted off to sleep.

The bright light on my face woke me up. For a minute I forgot everything.

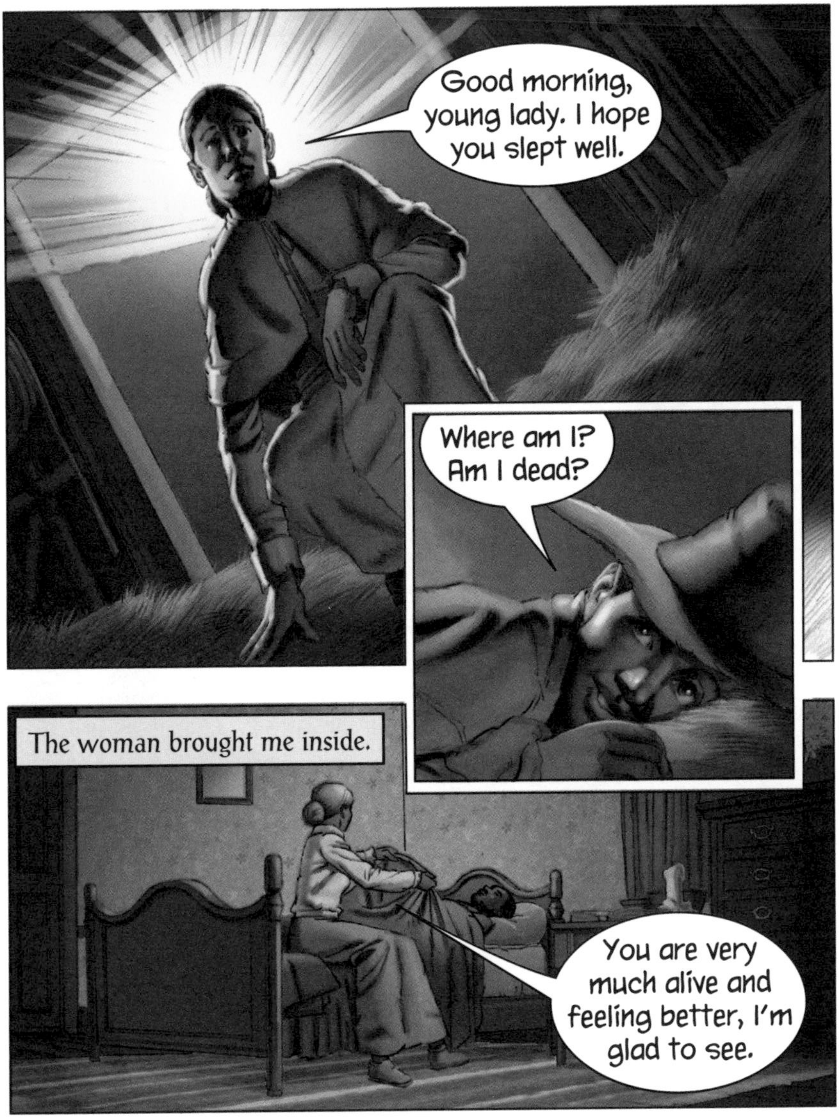
Good morning, young lady. I hope you slept well.
Where am I? Am I dead?
The woman brought me inside.
You are very much alive and feeling better, I'm glad to see.

It was the Quaker lady! She dressed me in a nice clean nightgown and put me to bed under a soft quilt. Nobody except my momma had ever been so kind to me before.

"When you feel better, come downstairs to the kitchen. I have breakfast for you," she said.

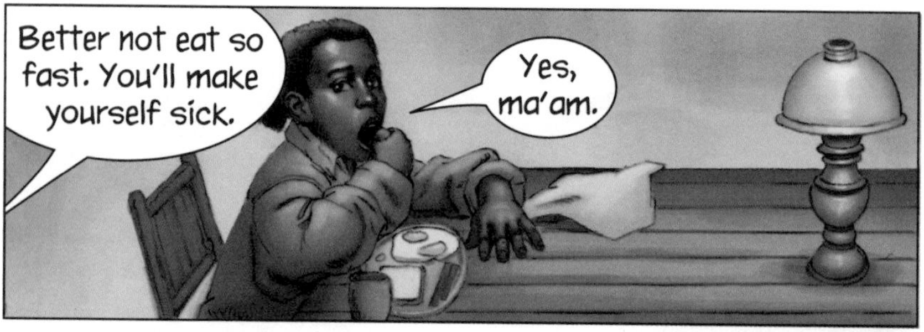
Better not eat so fast. You'll make yourself sick.
Yes, ma'am.

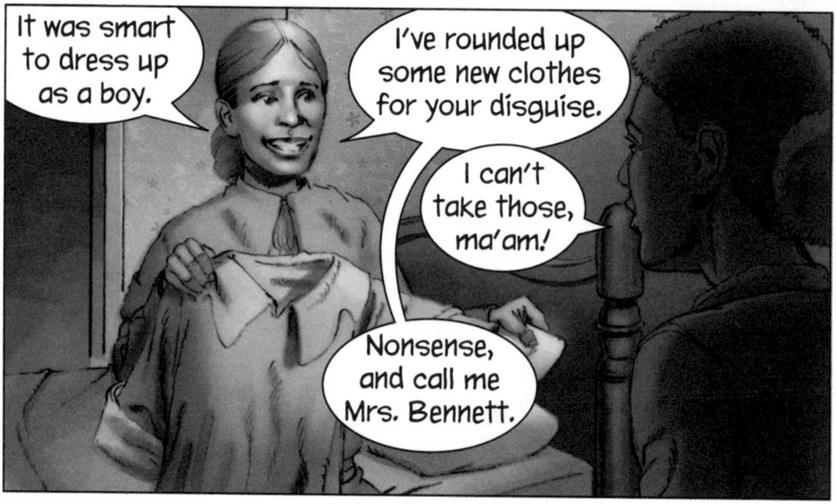
It was smart to dress up as a boy.
I've rounded up some new clothes for your disguise.
I can't take those, ma'am!
Nonsense, and call me Mrs. Bennett.

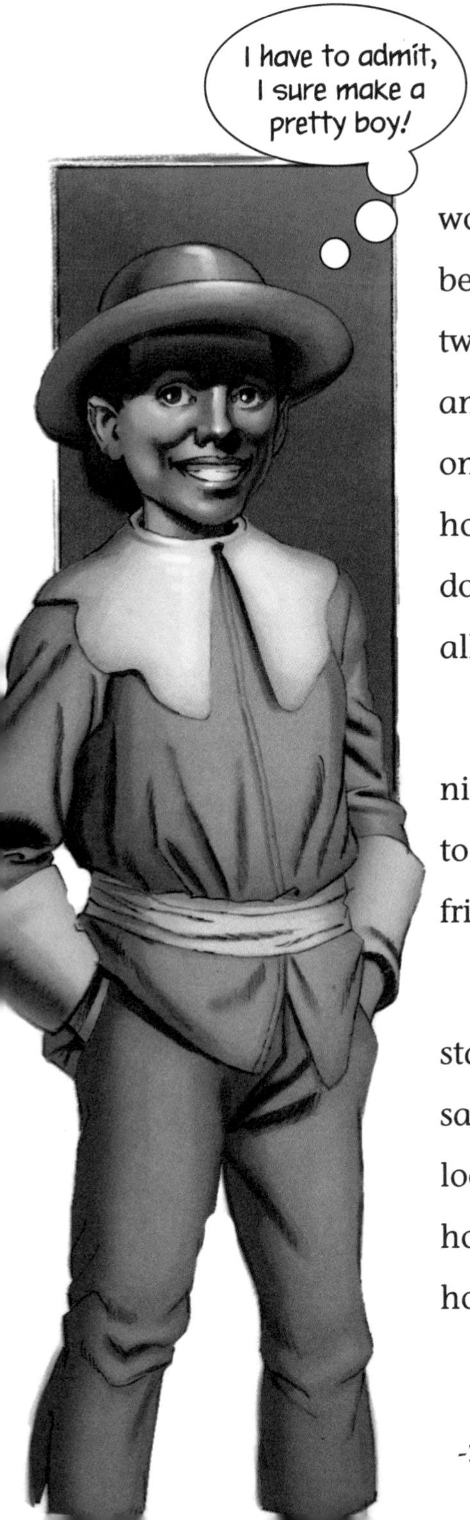
I have to admit, I sure make a pretty boy!

Mrs. Bennett's dinners would have made anybody better. I stayed with her for two days, until I felt strong and healthy. She never once asked who I was or how I wound up on her doorstep. But she knew all along.

Then, on the third night, Mrs. Bennett came to my room looking frightened.

"It's not safe for you to stay here any longer," she said. "The slave hunters are looking for you, and this house is too close to the house you escaped from."

I got scared again. Mrs. Bennett was going to throw me out, where I'd surely be captured by the slave hunters! But I shouldn't have doubted her. She had a plan.

"I'm drawing a map for you," she said. "It'll show you how to get to the next station on the Underground Railroad."

"You mean I'm going to ride on a train?" I asked.

"No, dear. The Underground Railroad isn't a real railroad at all," she replied.

Mrs. Bennett explained that the Underground Railroad was a series of houses where runaway slaves like me could find shelter with people who are against slavery. These people, called "conductors," wanted to help slaves escape. The house I was in was a station on the Underground Railroad, and Mrs. Bennett was a conductor!

That night, Mrs. Bennett wrapped up some food for my journey to the next station.

"Mrs. Bennett, would you tell my momma that you saw me, and that I'm all right?" I asked.

"Of course. Keep safe, dear," she replied.

Then it was time to go. I had to travel at night, following the creek. During the daytime, I would find a place to hide and rest. Sometimes I heard voices, but nobody ever found me.

One night, I heard a sound that I dreaded.

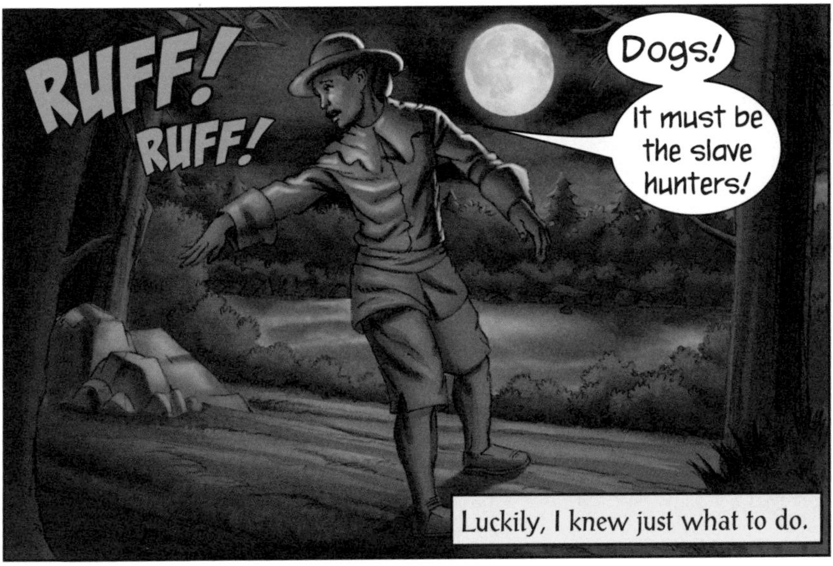
RUFF!
RUFF!
Dogs!
It must be the slave hunters!
Luckily, I knew just what to do.

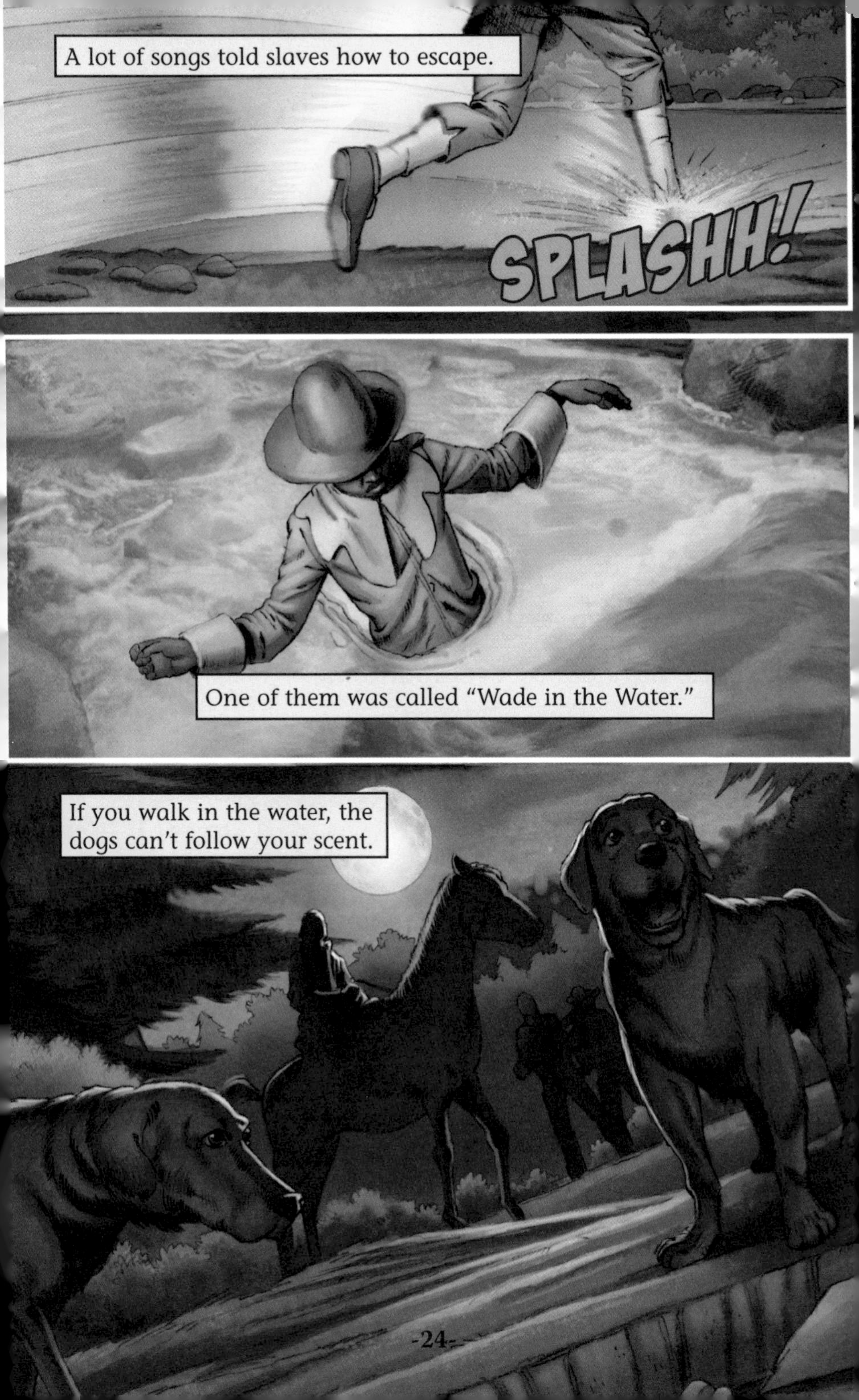
A lot of songs told slaves how to escape.
SPLASHH!
One of them was called "Wade in the Water."
If you walk in the water, the dogs can't follow your scent.

The water was up to my waist, and it was cold, but I knew I was safe. Soon I couldn't hear the dogs anymore. That meant they had lost my scent and turned back. As I slogged along, I sang to myself, real low, to keep up my spirits.

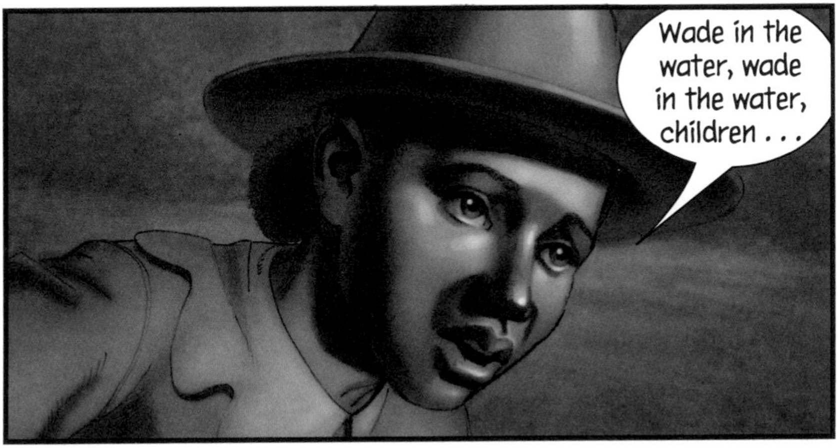
Wade in the water, wade in the water, children . . .

I waded through the murky water until the sun started to rise. Then I crawled onto the shore. I covered myself with leaves and ferns to stay warm and hidden.

That night, I set out again through the woods. After three days, I finally reached the next stop on the Underground Railroad.

# CHAPTER 3
# HARRIET'S HELP

At this stop, my conductor was Mr. Martin. I was surprised to find out that he wasn't a Quaker. It turned out that there were lots of people who were against slavery, not just Quakers. They were called abolitionists.

When I arrived, Mr. Martin introduced me to other runaway slaves. "Sarah, I'd like you to meet Jane and her children, Molly and John," he said.

Molly was about my age. She held her baby brother in her arms and smiled.

"Sarah? That's a funny name for a boy," she said, looking puzzled.

"I'm not a boy, silly! I'm in disguise," I said.

Just then, something terrible happened . . .

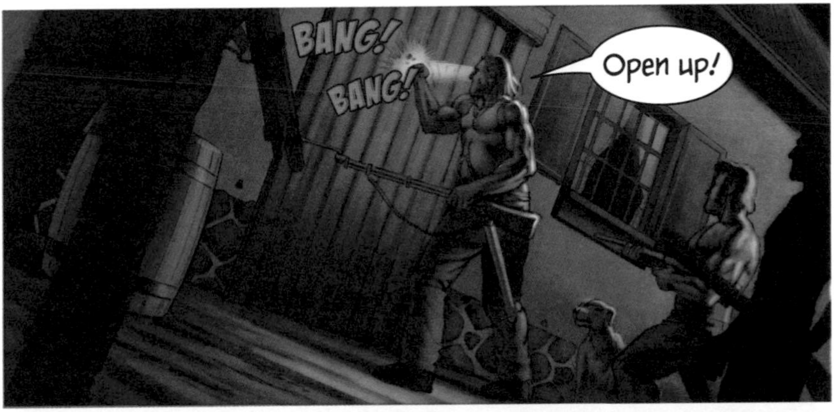
BANG!
BANG!
Open up!

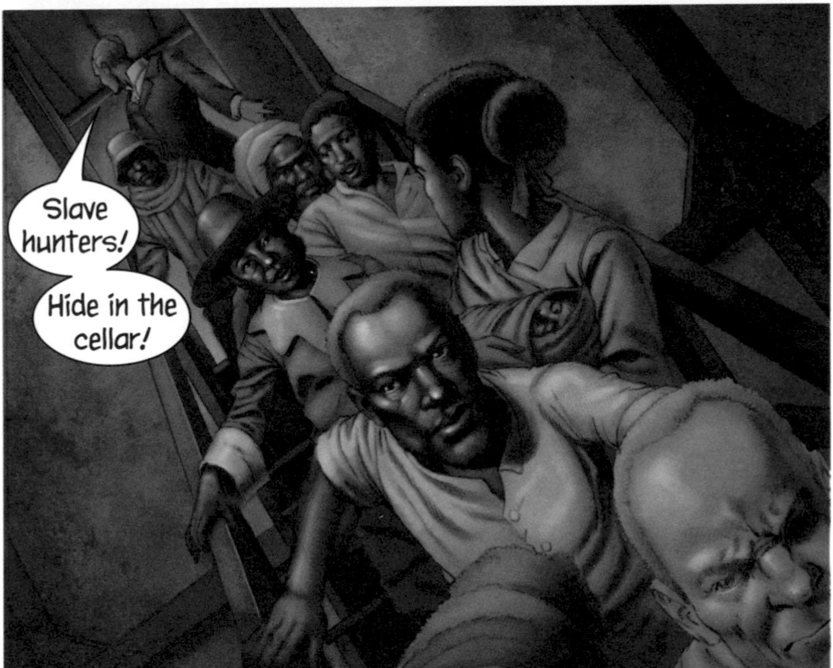
Slave hunters!
Hide in the cellar!

The dogs had picked up my scent after all!

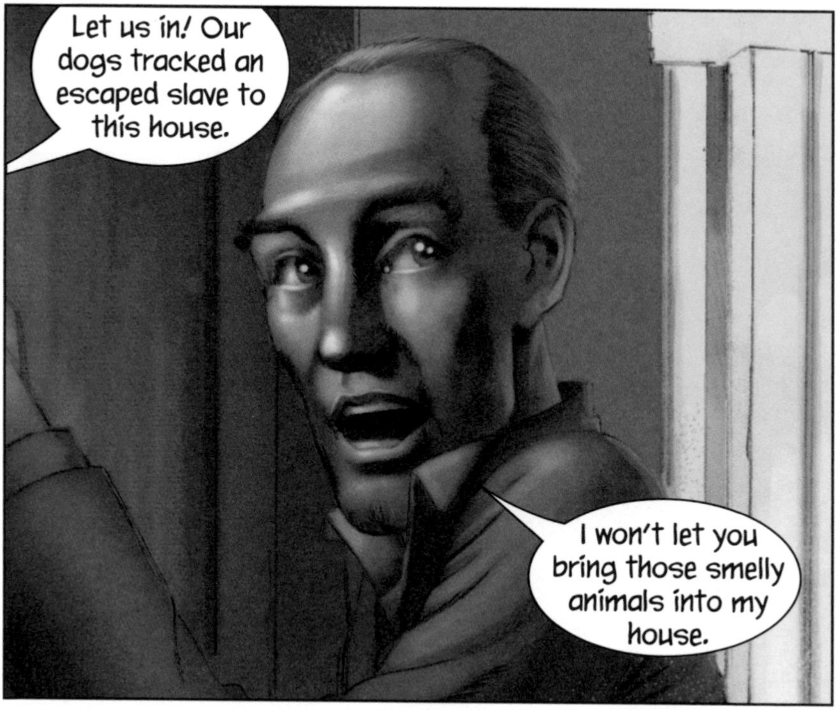
Let us in! Our dogs tracked an escaped slave to this house.
I won't let you bring those smelly animals into my house.

Mr. Martin kept the men standing outside as long as he could, to give us time to hide in the root cellar. We hid behind sacks of flour and bushels of apples and carrots.

From our hiding place in the cellar, we could hear the sound of the slave hunters' heavy boots as they tore the house apart, looking for us. But at least Mr. Martin made them leave their dogs outside, and that was lucky.

I could hear one of the slave hunters yelling at Mr. Martin. "You are a known abolitionist," he said. "You must be hiding the escaped slave somewhere."

"Maybe they're in the cellar," the other slave hunter said.

"There's nothing down there but our stored food," Mr. Martin lied.

We'll see about that.

As they stomped down the stairs, I prayed they could not hear the beating of my heart.

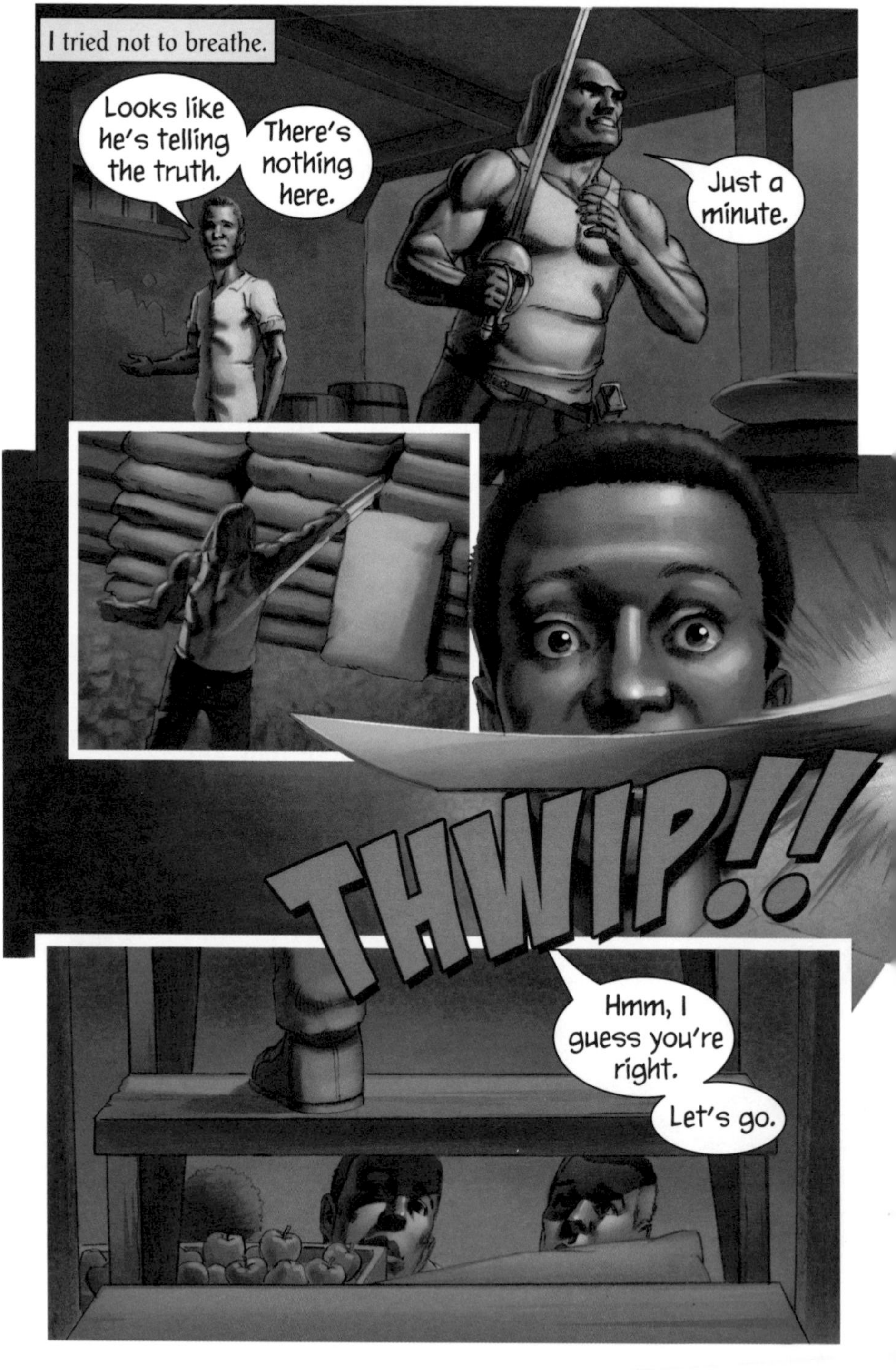
I tried not to breathe.
Looks like he's telling the truth.
There's nothing here.
Just a minute.
THWIP!!
Hmm, I guess you're right.
Let's go.

We heard the slave hunters slam the door as they went out, but we still didn't move. We stayed behind the sacks until Mr. Martin called us.

"They're gone. You can come out!" he yelled.

Molly and I hugged each other. We were laughing and crying at the same time.

"Oh, Molly, if they had caught us it would've been all my fault!" I sobbed. "Those dogs were following my scent."

"Don't be silly, Sarah. It could have been any one of us," she said.

During the next few days, Molly and I became friends. I had never had a friend my own age before. We promised that we would be like sisters, and we would never part.

The next night there was another knock at the door. We froze. Had the slave hunters come back?

Mr. Martin slowly approached the door. He was ready to tell us to hide again in the cellar.

"Who is it?" he asked.

"It's a friend with friends," a woman on the other side of the door replied.

We didn't have to be afraid. That phrase was secret code that the conductors understood. It meant that the person at the door was bringing escaped slaves.

Mr. Martin opened the door.

Harriet Tubman!

All of us slaves had heard of Harriet Tubman. They called her the Moses of her people. Just like Moses, she had led hundreds of slaves to the promised land of freedom in the Northern states.

Harriet brought two men with her, runaway slaves like us. Abel and Sam were field hands. They had worked under a brutal master. He treated them so harshly that they feared he would kill them if they didn't escape. I could see that they both had scars from being whipped.

Harriet didn't want to wait long, in case the slave hunters came back. Our small group set out the next night. Abel and Sam looked like they were in pretty bad shape. I worried about them being able to make the journey.

Sure enough, we had been walking through the woods for only a few hours when suddenly Abel fell down. He wouldn't get up.

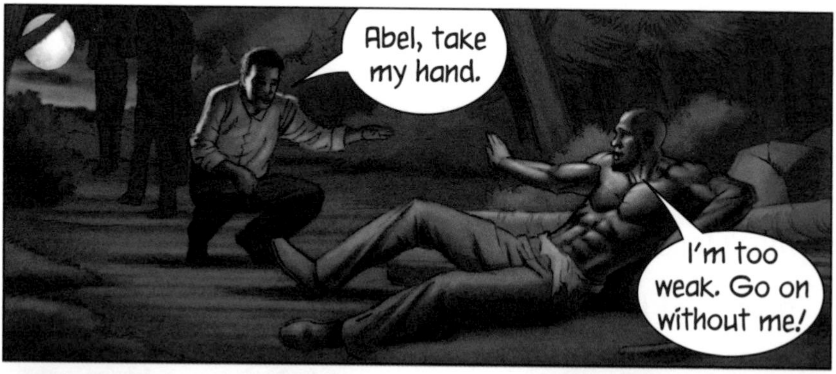
Abel, take my hand.
I'm too weak. Go on without me!

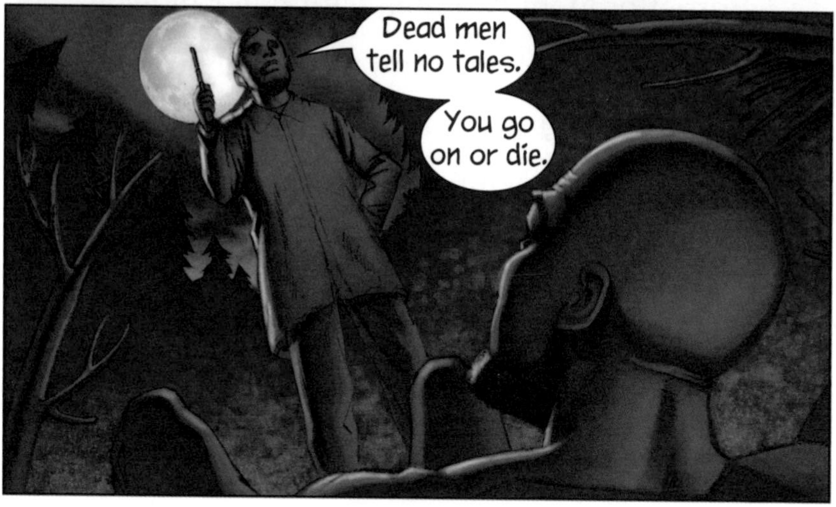
Dead men tell no tales.
You go on or die.

I don't know if Harriet would have shot Abel, but what she said worked. Abel got up and walked the rest of the way with us. If he had stayed behind and been caught, the slave hunters might have forced him to tell them all he knew about the Underground Railroad. He could have put hundreds of people in danger.

# CHAPTER 4
# MANY THOUSANDS GONE

During the next several days, we continued on our journey to the North. Sometimes we traveled on foot. Other times, members of the Underground Railroad would cover us up and let us ride a few miles in the back of their wagons. No matter how we traveled, I always worried about being caught.

Three weeks after I had escaped, we reached the promised land of Philadelphia, Pennsylvania. The city was even bigger than I had expected. As we walked down the crowded streets, something surprised me even more.

"Look at all those black folks on the streets," I exclaimed. "They're just as free as the whites."

In Philadelphia, we parted ways with Sam and Abel. They went to stay in one house, and I went with Molly's family to another. We stayed with the Rosses, a family of free black people.

As we settled in, Molly's mother made me new dresses, prettier than anything I had ever worn. I felt like a princess!

My joyful moment was soon interrupted. Harriet Tubman came to say good-bye. She was off to lead more people to the promised land.

I wondered if I would ever see her again.

A few days later, Molly and I found work, so that we could give some money to the kind people who sheltered us. We were hired by a big hotel to clean the rooms and wash the floors.

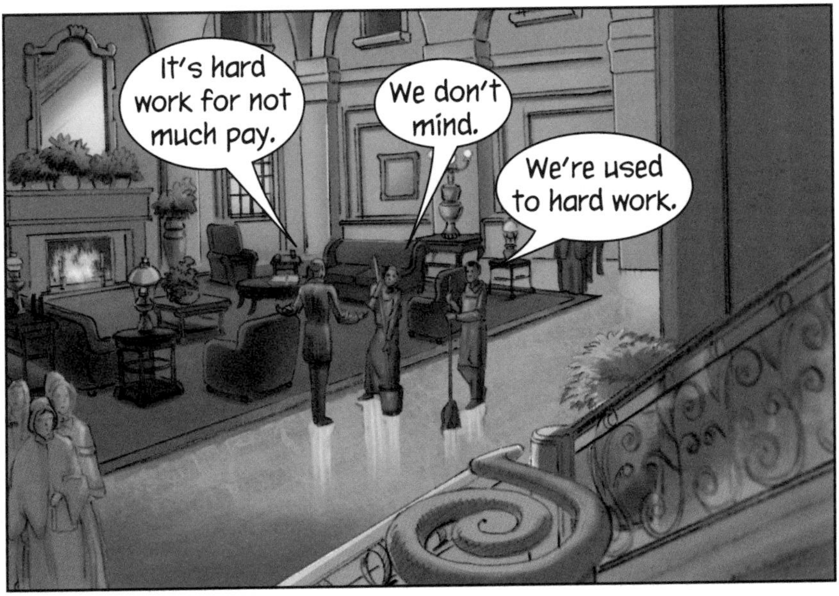
It's hard work for not much pay.
We don't mind.
We're used to hard work.

This time we were working for ourselves, not any master. I thought life was perfect, but I should have known better. One day Molly and I were scrubbing the floor in the hotel lobby. Suddenly, I heard a voice I had hoped never to hear again.

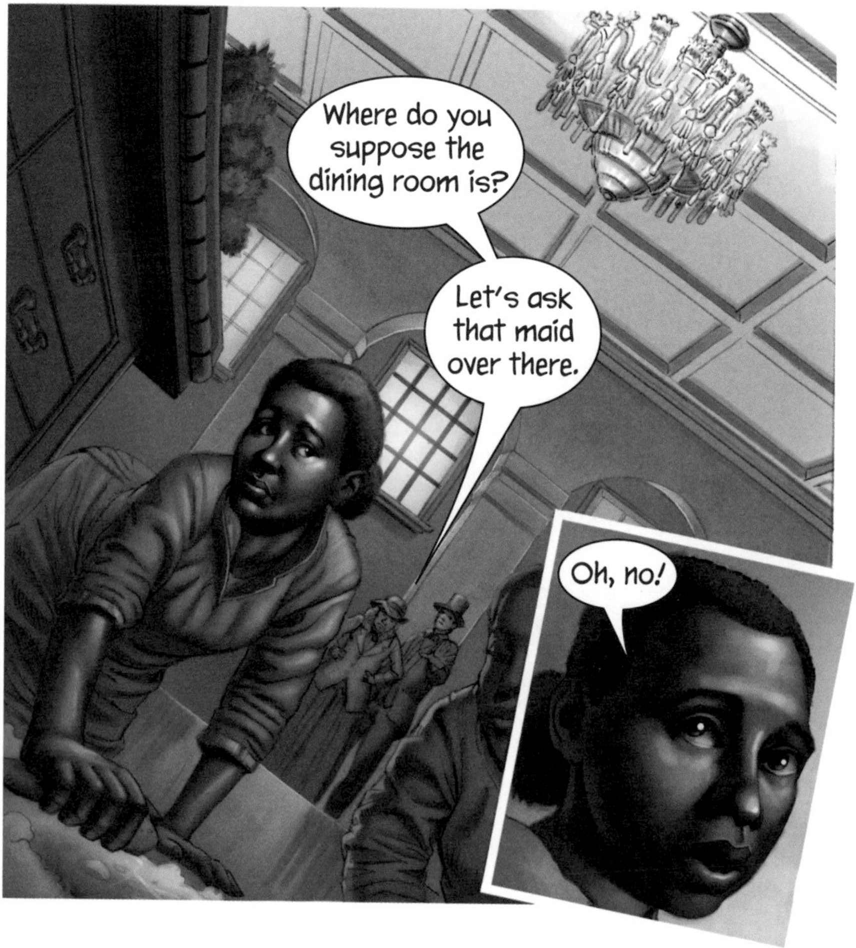
Where do you suppose the dining room is?
Let's ask that maid over there.
Oh, no!

It was my old owners, the Marlows! I kept my head down and pretended I didn't hear them.

"See here, girl, where is the dining room?" Mr. Marlow raised his voice, which I'd heard him do plenty of times before.

"What's the matter, are you deaf?" Mrs. Marlow added. I tried to keep my head down, but she pulled me toward her face.

"Eek!" she screamed. "Look, James! That's our escaped slave, Sarah!"

They both stared at me, looking even more angry than the day I left. I suddenly remembered what Mr. Marlow had said that day, "We'll give her the whipping she deserves." I couldn't even imagine what he would do to me now.

"Quick, James, get that little thief before she runs away again!" Mrs. Marlow yelled at her husband.

As she continued to scream, the people in the hotel lobby started to rush toward us. I had to do something fast. But what? I looked at Molly, who was standing beside me, holding the pail of soapy water. She had read my mind.

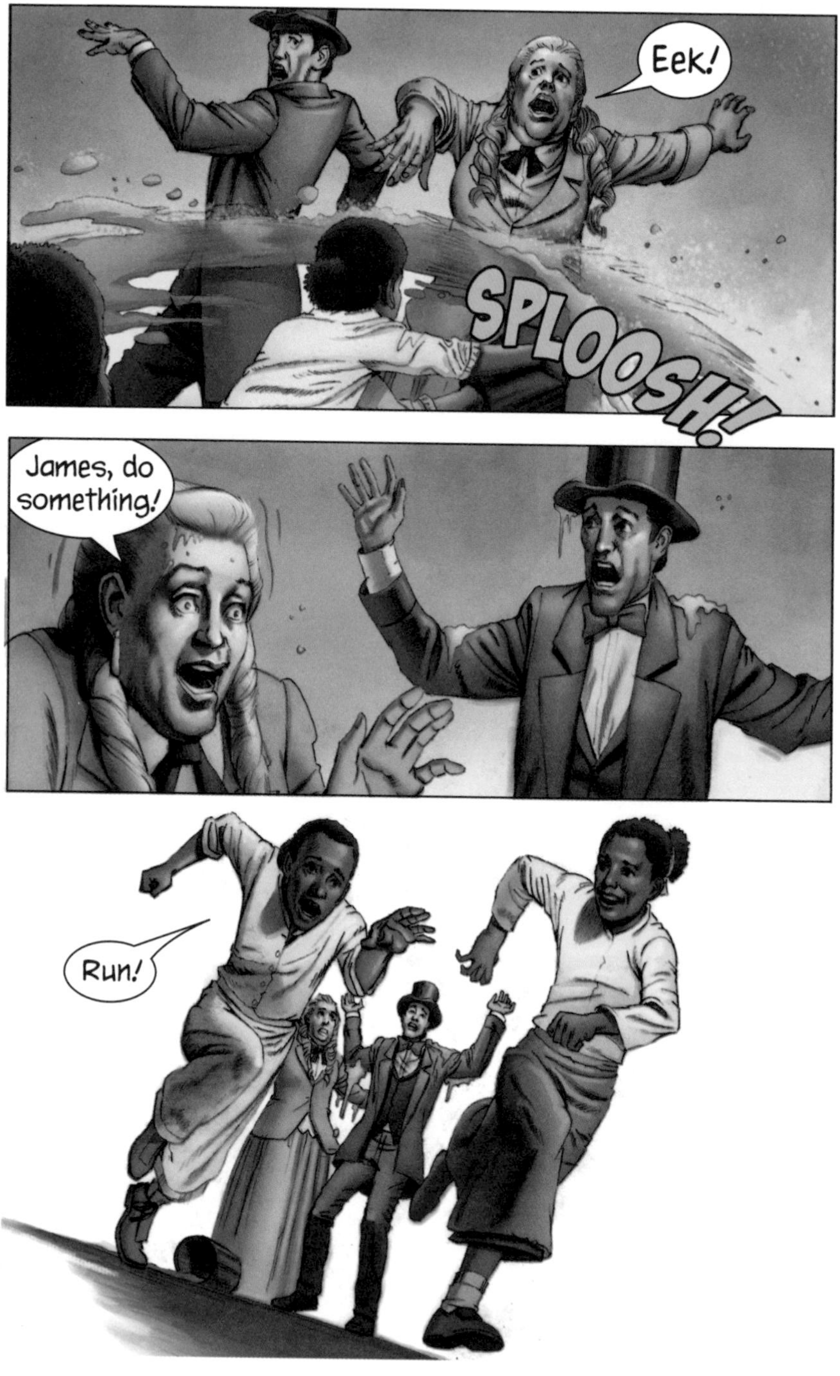
Eek!
SPLOOSH!
James, do something!
Run!

The situation was serious.

"You're not safe here anymore, Sarah. Now that your old owners know that you're in Philadelphia, they'll tell the police to look for you," said Mr. Ross.

Mr. Ross told me about a law called the Fugitive Slave Act. The law said that if runaway slaves were caught, even in a free state, they would have to go back to their old owners in the South.

"We're breaking the law by hiding you, and if you are caught, we'll be punished," he said.

I would have to go to Canada, the only place where I would be safe.

I was tired of leaving the people I loved, but I had to go. Every minute I stayed there, Molly and her mother and baby brother were in danger.

## CHAPTER 5
# FREE AT LAST!

The next morning, Mr. Ross hitched up the horses and prepared the wagon for the ride to the train station. I said good-bye to my friend.

"Oh Molly, I'll miss you more than anything!"

"Promise you'll write as soon as you reach Canada," Molly said as I boarded the wagon.

"I promise," I said.

Mr. Ross yelled "Giddyup" to the horses, and the wagon started down the dusty road. As much as I wanted to look back, I knew I couldn't.

When we arrived at the train station, Mr. Ross bought me two tickets. One ticket for the train to New York, and the other for the boat to Canada.

"When you get to New York, there will be a man waiting to take you to the boat," Mr. Ross said. "But nobody can come with you on this part of the trip, Sarah."

Again, I had to say good-bye. I waved to Mr. Ross until he rounded the corner at the end of the platform and left my sight. I looked around the station. Plenty of people were waiting in line, buying tickets, and boarding trains. But at that moment, I realized that I was on my own again. The rest of the journey was up to me.

After only a few minutes of waiting for my train, I saw a policeman at the other end of the station platform. I hoped he wasn't looking for me!

I tried to look invisible, but the policeman kept walking closer. Instead of waiting around to get caught, I picked up my suitcase and started to walk away slowly. After a moment, I looked over my shoulder. He was still there, and now he was walking even faster!

The policeman had a piece of paper that he kept looking at. Suddenly, he held up the paper and yelled. "Hey, you! Stop right there!"

My eyes caught a glimpse of the piece of paper the policeman was holding. My heart stopped! The paper said, "Wanted, runaway slave." The policeman was looking for me!

There was only one thing to do.

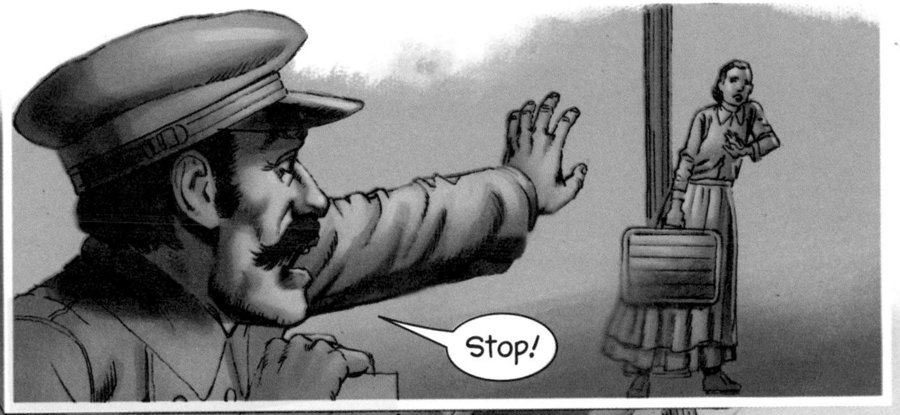
Stop!

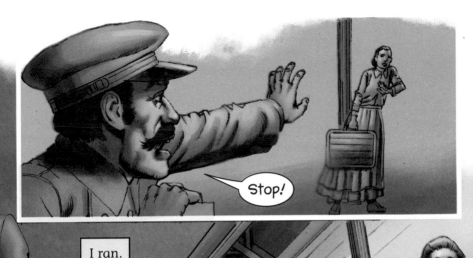

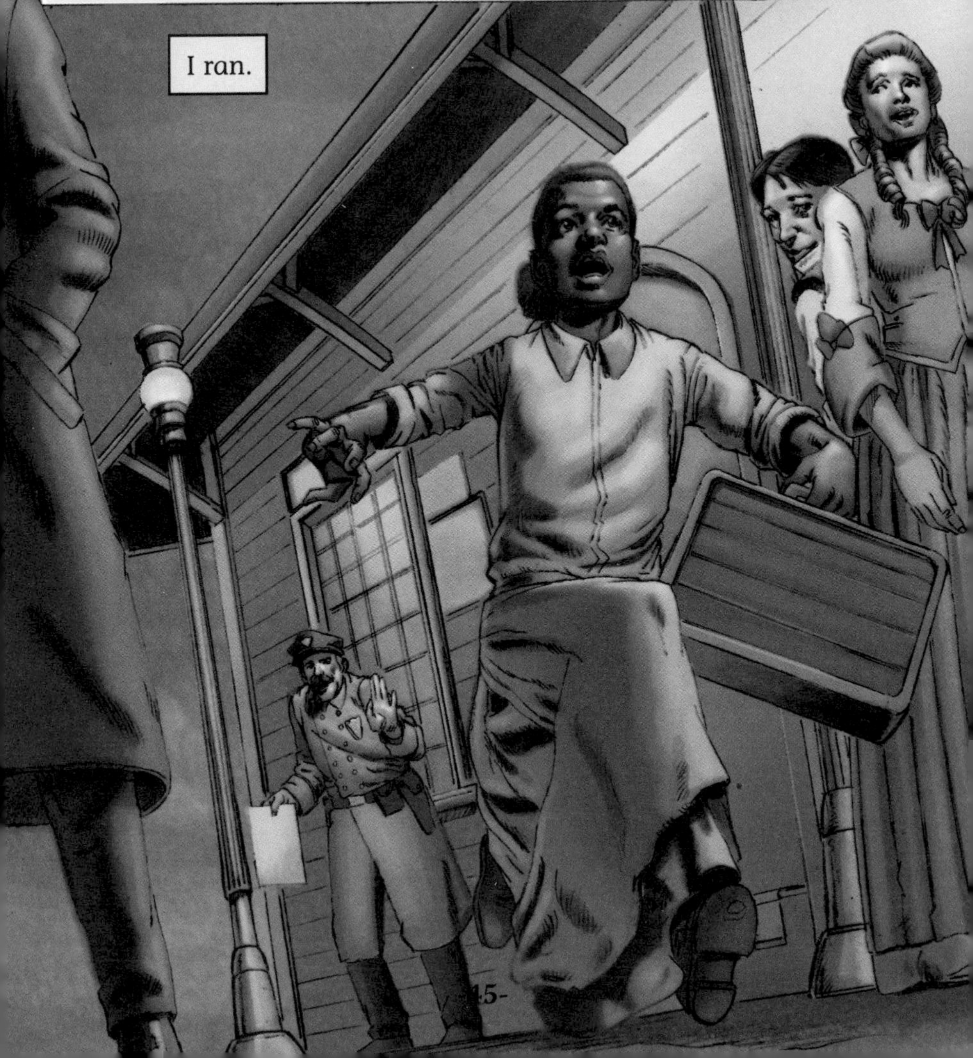
I ran.

There was a man standing up ahead who looked familiar. Where had I seen him before? Then I remembered. It was the peddler, Elijah Levy, the man who had told me about the Quaker lady! Would he remember me?

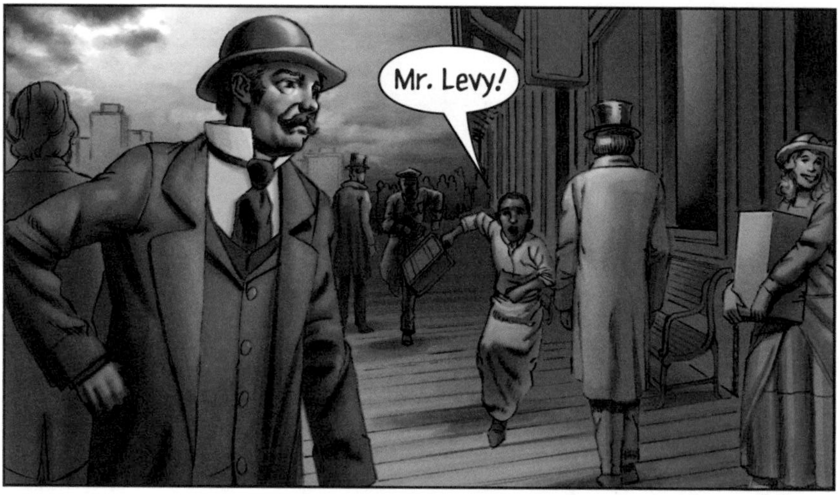
Mr. Levy!

In a second, I hatched a plan. But would Mr. Levy understand? Would he play along?

"I'm sorry I'm late, Mr. Levy." I said, running up to him. "I waited on the platform, like you said, but I was on the wrong side. Here are your samples." I handed him my suitcase.

Mr. Levy looked puzzled. But when the officer came running up behind me, Mr. Levy finally understood my plan. I was pretending to be his servant!

"So there you are! You waited on the wrong side," Mr. Levy said, going along with the plan.

He then turned and faced the policeman. "What seems to be the problem, officer?" he said.

"Is this your servant, sir?" the policeman asked while trying to catch his breath.

"She surely is, although sometimes I wish she wasn't. Girl can't even fetch my bag without getting lost," Mr. Levy said.

The officer finally caught his breath and stood up straight. He must have known that Mr. Levy was lying. I had traveled too far and come too close to freedom for it all to end like this.

Then the officer said something I didn't expect.

"I'm terribly sorry, sir," he mumbled, looking somewhat embarrassed. "I thought she was someone else."

The officer walked away, scratching his head and looking again at the wanted poster. At the end of the platform, the conductor shouted, "All aboard!"

Mr. Levy grabbed my hand and pulled me quickly onto the train. The doors closed and the train started moving. I was safe!

"Mr. Levy, you did remember me," I said.

"Of course, Sarah. I'm glad to see that you listened to what I said," he told me.

Finally I was on my way to freedom, on a real railroad this time. Someday, I promised myself, I'll be just like Harriet Tubman. I'll come back and rescue my mother. And I'll go back to Philadelphia and see my best friend Molly again, when everyone in this land is finally free.

# ABOUT THE AUTHOR

Trina Robbins grew up in Brooklyn, New York. Her mother, a second-grade schoolteacher, taught her to read at age four. She says, "It is the greatest gift anyone has ever given me." Robbins turned her love of books into a lifelong career. For more than 30 years, she has been writing graphic novels and children's books. Her work includes comics such as *Wonder Woman* and *Powerpuff Girls,* as well as *GoGirl!,* her own graphic novel series for girls.

# ABOUT THE ILLUSTRATOR

Jason Millet has been a freelance illustrator and cartoonist for more than 10 years. He has worked for a wide variety of publishing and advertising companies, including DC Comics, Devil's Due Publishing, Major League Baseball, Wizards of the Coast, Disney, and Choose Your Own Adventures.

# GLOSSARY

**abolitionist** (ab-uh-LISH-uh-nist)—someone who worked to abolish slavery before the U.S. Civil War

**ashamed** (uh-SHAIMED)—feeling embarrassed or guilty about something

**cellar** (SEL-ur)—a room below the ground, which was often used for storing food and supplies

**disguise** (diss-GIZE)—a costume or outfit meant to hide someone's identity, or who they actually are

**gourd** (GORD)—a type of fruit similar to a pumpkin or squash

**Quaker** (KWAY-kur)—a member of a Christian religious group known as the Society of Friends

**servant** (SUR-vuhnt)—someone who cooks, cleans, and does other household chores for another

**slave** (SLAYV)—someone who is owned by another person and is often forced to do their work

**stable** (STAY-buhl)—a building for horses, cattle, and other farm animals

**wade** (WAYD)—to walk through water

# ABOUT SLAVERY AND THE UNDERGROUND RAILROAD

In the mid-1800s, Southern states allowed slavery while Northern states did not. This border between free and slave states is often called the Mason–Dixon Line, which runs between Maryland and Pennsylvania.

Before the Civil War (1861–1865), more than 1,000 slaves escaped from the South every year. Many of these slaves went to Northern states where slavery was illegal.

Even slaves that made it to Northern states weren't always safe. A law called the Fugitive Slave Act allowed slave owners to capture runaway slaves and bring them back to the South. To avoid being caught, many slaves fled all the way to Canada.

Harriet Tubman (1820–1913) was a real conductor on the Underground Railroad. She made 19 trips to the South to rescue more than 300 people from slavery, including her own parents.

Before she could help others, Harriet Tubman had to escape slavery herself in 1849. For many years after, she was at risk of being caught. In fact, her owner posted a $40,000 reward for her capture in 1856.

The argument over slavery helped lead to the U.S. Civil War in 1861. Northern states fought against Southern states. In April 1865, the North defeated the South, and the war finally ended.

Soon after the Civil War, Congress passed the 13th Amendment. This addition to the U.S. Constitution ended slavery in America.

# DISCUSSION QUESTIONS

1. Sarah had to leave her mother in the South in order to escape. Why do you believe she made this decision? Do you think that you could have made the same choice?

2. Name at least three people in the story that helped Sarah on her journey to freedom. How did each person help her and why?

3. How did songs help Sarah and others escape from slavery? Use examples from the story to support your answer.

# WRITING PROMPTS

1. This story is known as historical fiction. The historical event is true, but the characters and story line is fiction. Choose your favorite historical event. Then make up a story that happens on that day.

2. Choose one of the other characters from this book, such as Mr. Levy, Molly, or Harriet Tubman. Then write your own story about that person.

3. At the end of the book, Sarah says that she will return to the South and rescue her mother. Write your own story describing this adventure.

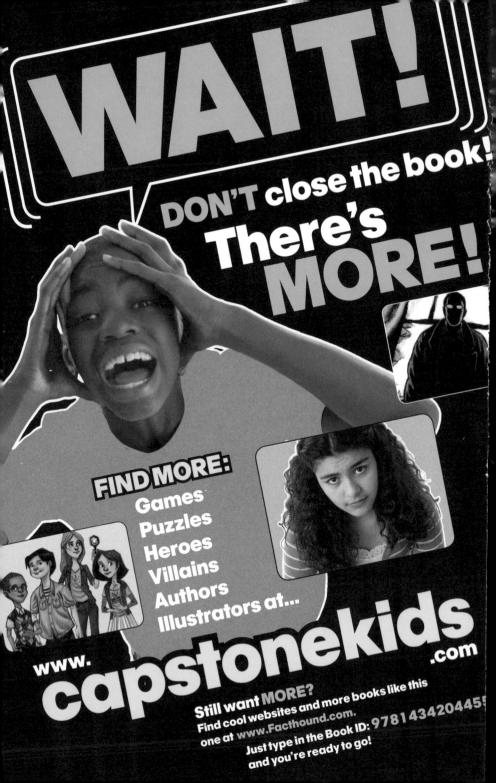

# A NOTE TO PARENTS

## Reading Aloud with Your Child

*Research shows that reading books aloud is the single most valuable support parents can provide in helping children learn to read.*

- Be a ham! The more enthusiasm you display, the more your child will enjoy the book.
- Run your finger underneath the words as you read to signal that the print carries the story.
- Leave time for examining the illustrations more closely; encourage your child to find things in the pictures.
- Invite your youngster to join in whenever there's a repeated phrase in the text.
- Link up events in the book with similar events in your child's life.
- If your child asks a question, stop and answer it. The book can be a means to learning more about your child's thoughts.

## Listening to Your Child Read Aloud

*The support of your attention and praise is absolutely crucial to your child's continuing efforts to learn to read.*

- If your child is learning to read and asks for a word, give it immediately so that the meaning of the story is not interrupted. DO NOT ask your child to sound out the word.
- On the other hand, if your child initiates the act of sounding out, don't intervene.
- If your child is reading along and makes what is called a miscue, listen for the sense of the miscue. If the word "road" is substituted for the word "street," for instance, no meaning is lost. Don't stop the reading for a correction.
- If the miscue makes no sense (for example, "horse" for "house"), ask your child to reread the sentence because you're not sure you understand what's just been read.
- Above all else, enjoy your child's growing command of print and make sure you give lots of praise. *You are your child's first teacher—and the most important one. Praise from you is critical for further risk-taking and learning.*

—Priscilla Lynch
Ph.D., New York University
Educational Consultant

To Jordan
—G.M.

To Taylor Duffy and Austin Geary,
in hopes that this book will comfort them
if and when they see their first spots.
—B.L.

ISBN 0-590-50930-6

Text copyright © 1992 by Grace Maccarone.
Illustrations copyright © 1992 by Betsy Lewin.
All rights reserved. Published by Scholastic Inc.
HELLO READER!, CARTWHEEL BOOKS, and the CARTWHEEL BOOKS
logo are registered trademarks of Scholastic Inc.
The HELLO READER! logo is a trademark of Scholastic Inc.

12  11  10  9  8  7  6  5                3                7  8  9/9  0/0

Printed in the U.S.A.                                              37

# Itchy, Itchy Chicken Pox

by Grace Maccarone
Illustrated by Betsy Lewin

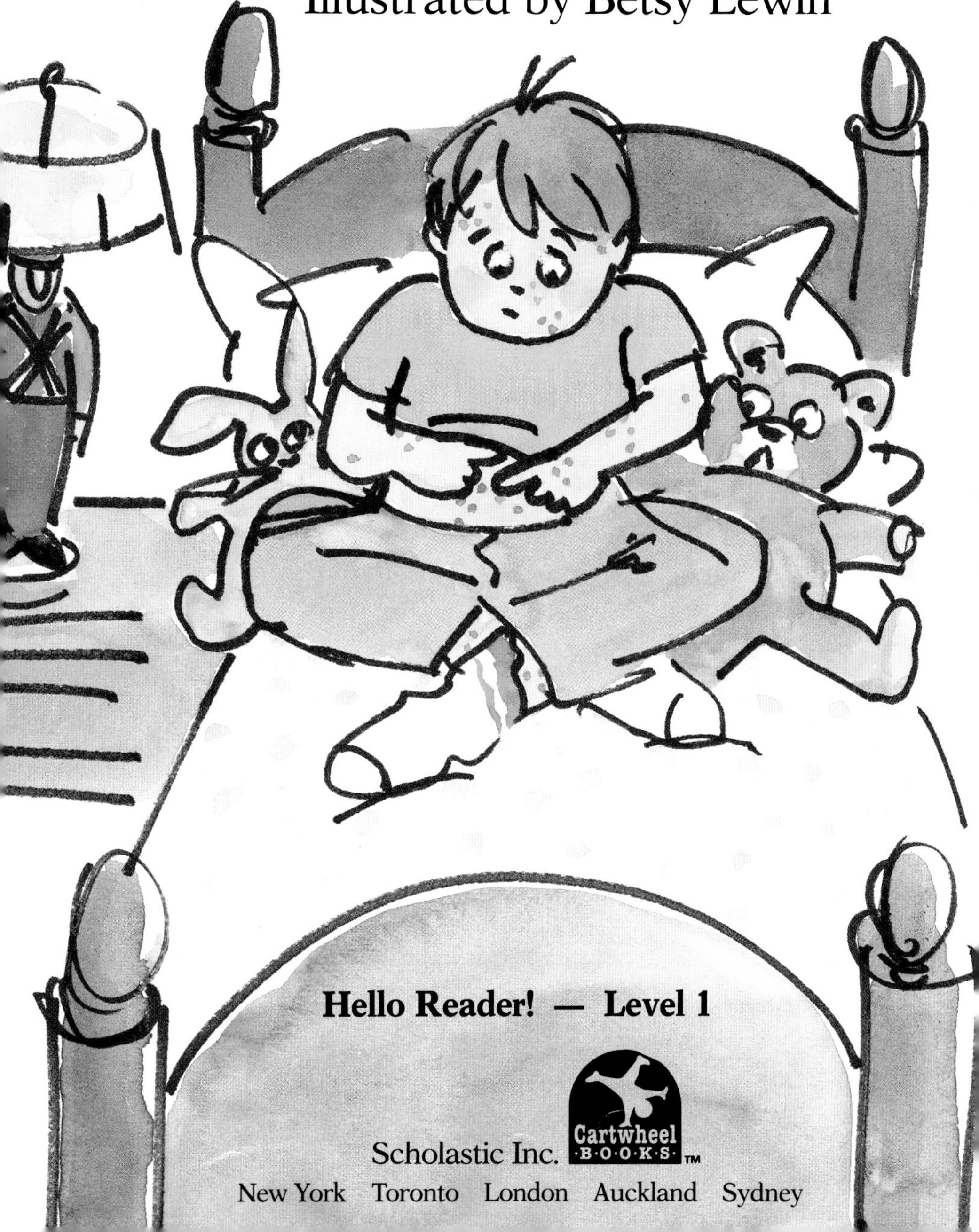

Hello Reader! — Level 1

Cartwheel BOOKS™
Scholastic Inc.
New York Toronto London Auckland Sydney

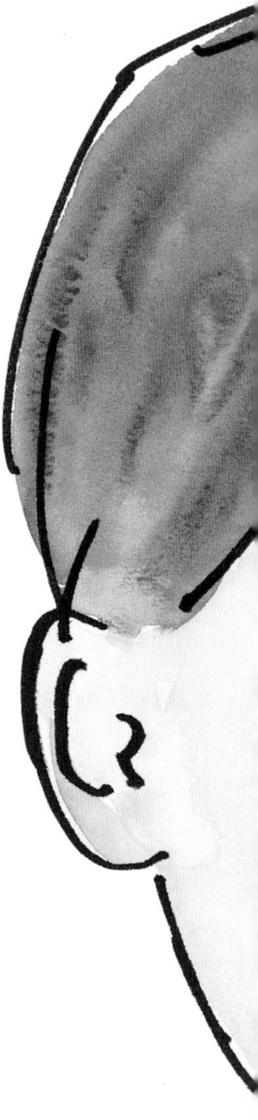

A spot.
A spot.
Another spot.

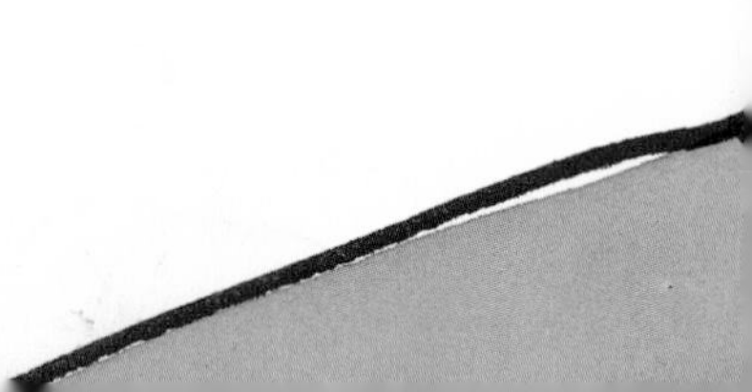

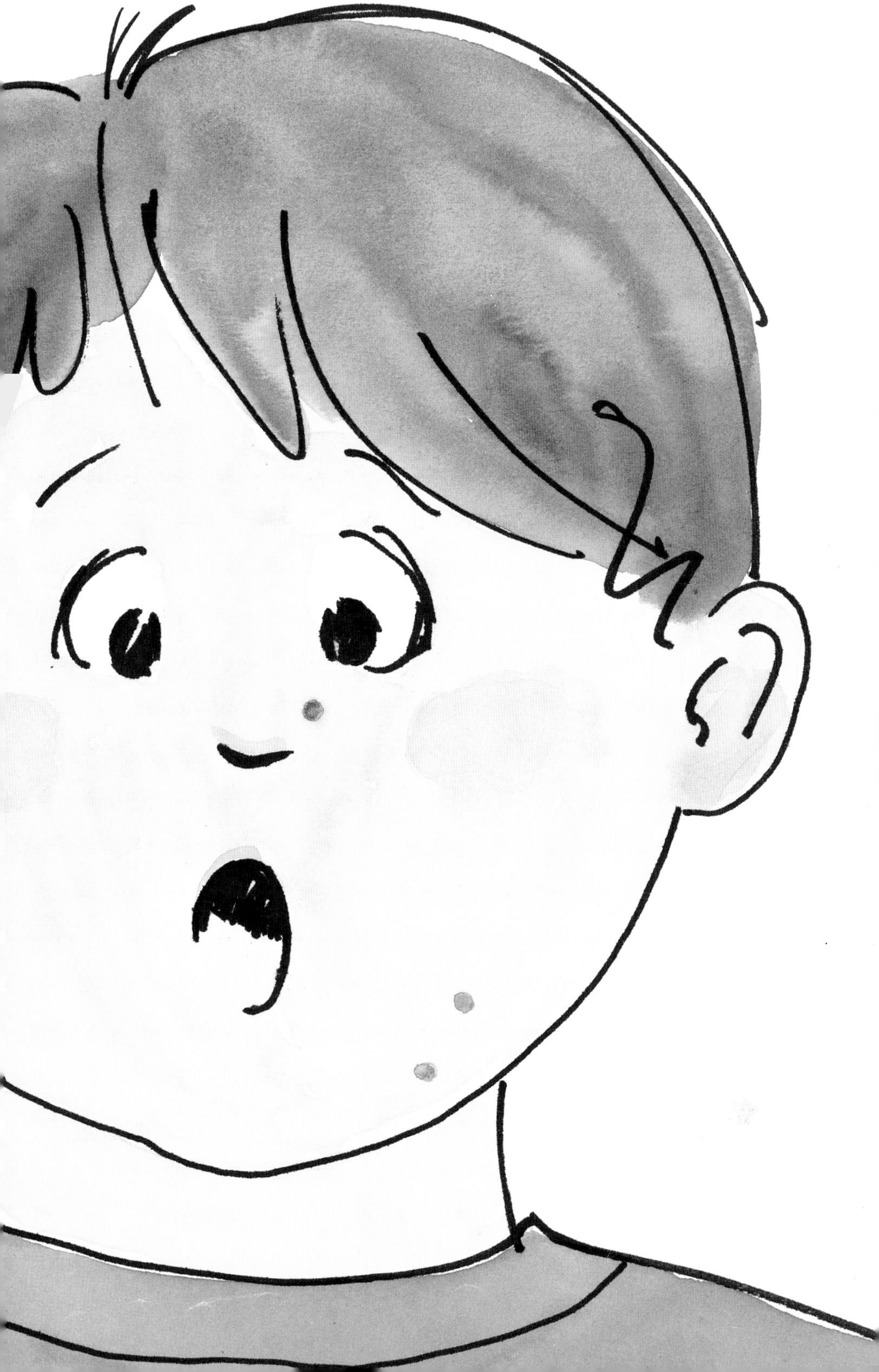

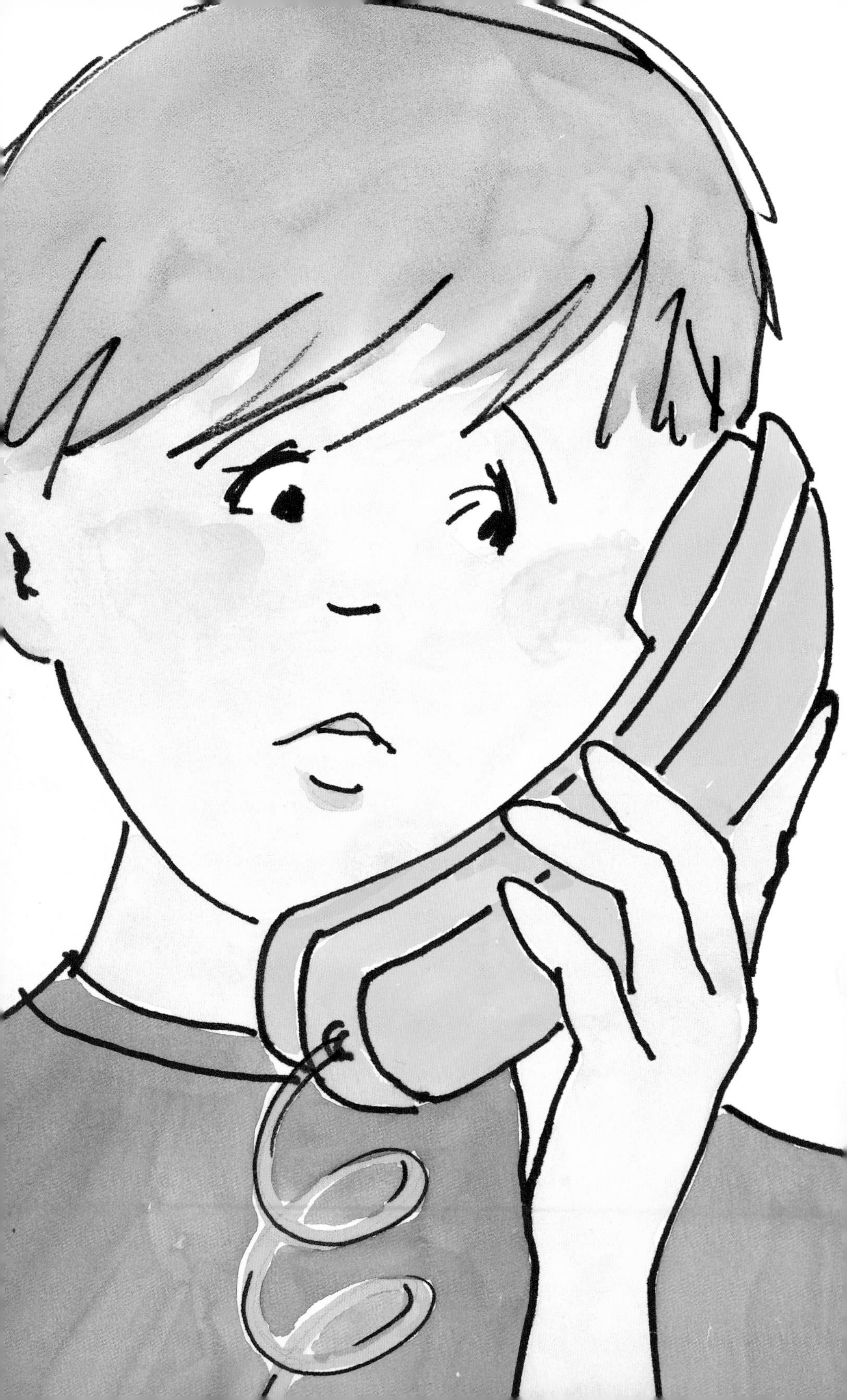

Uh-oh!
Chicken pox!

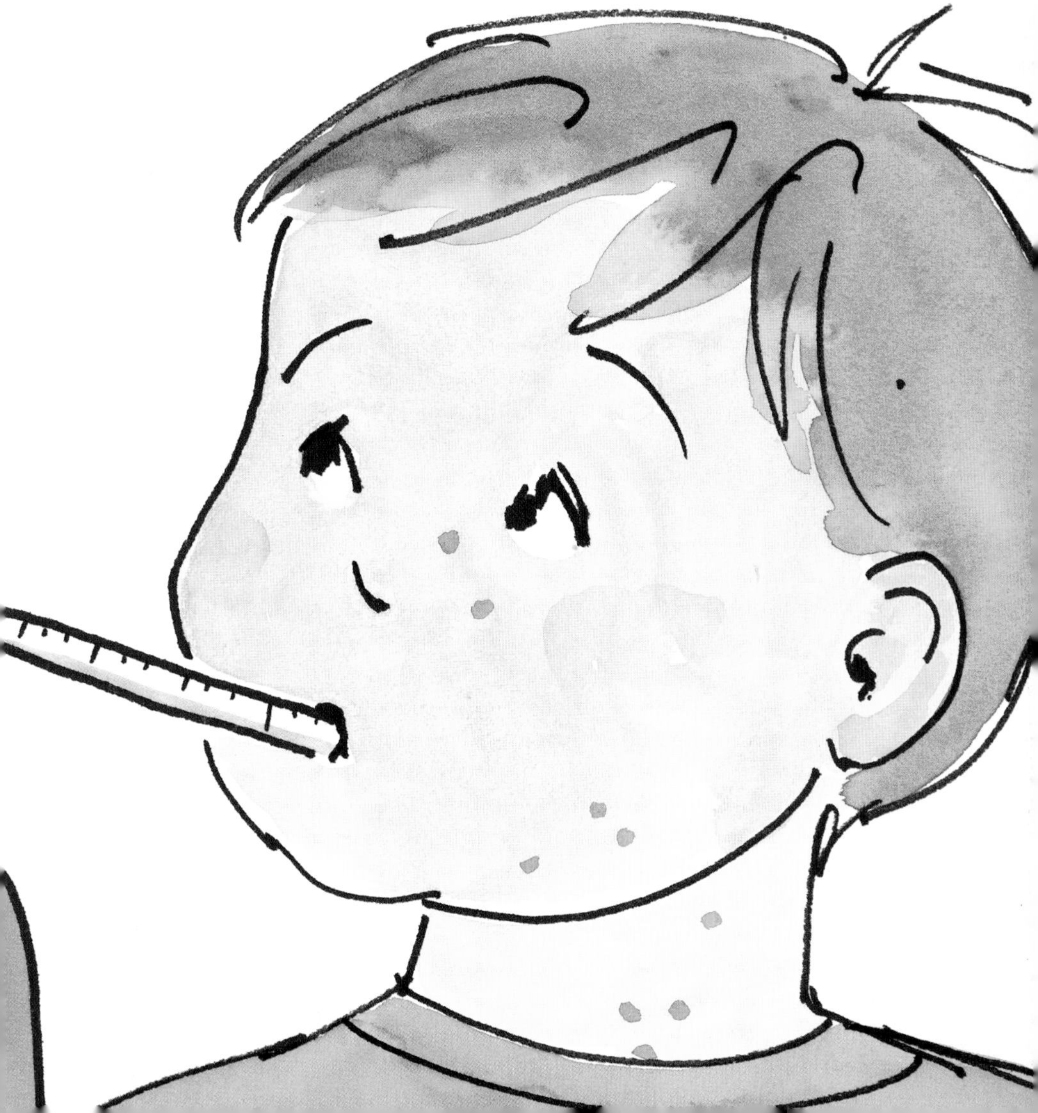

Under my shirt.
Under my socks.

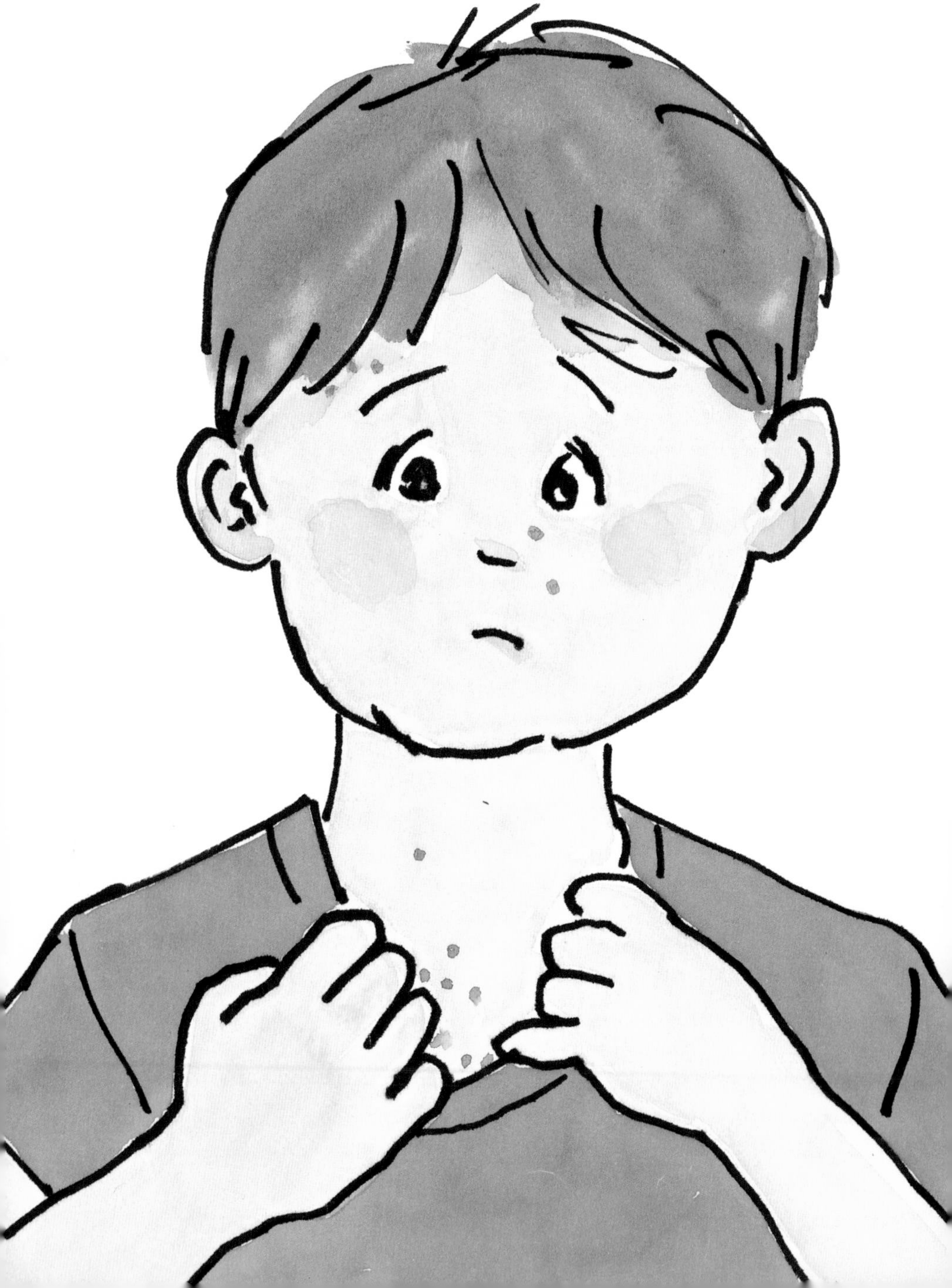

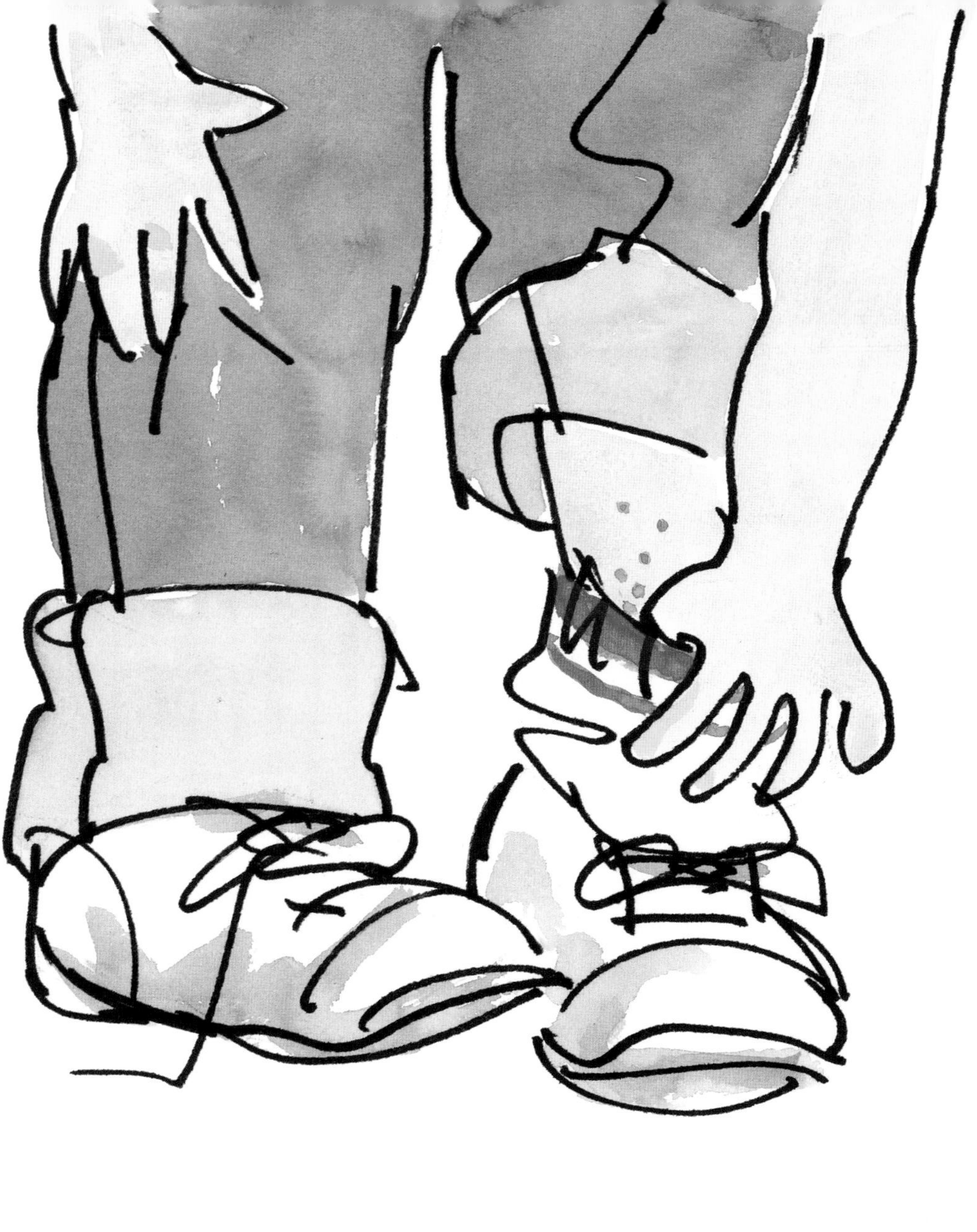

Itchy, itchy
chicken pox.

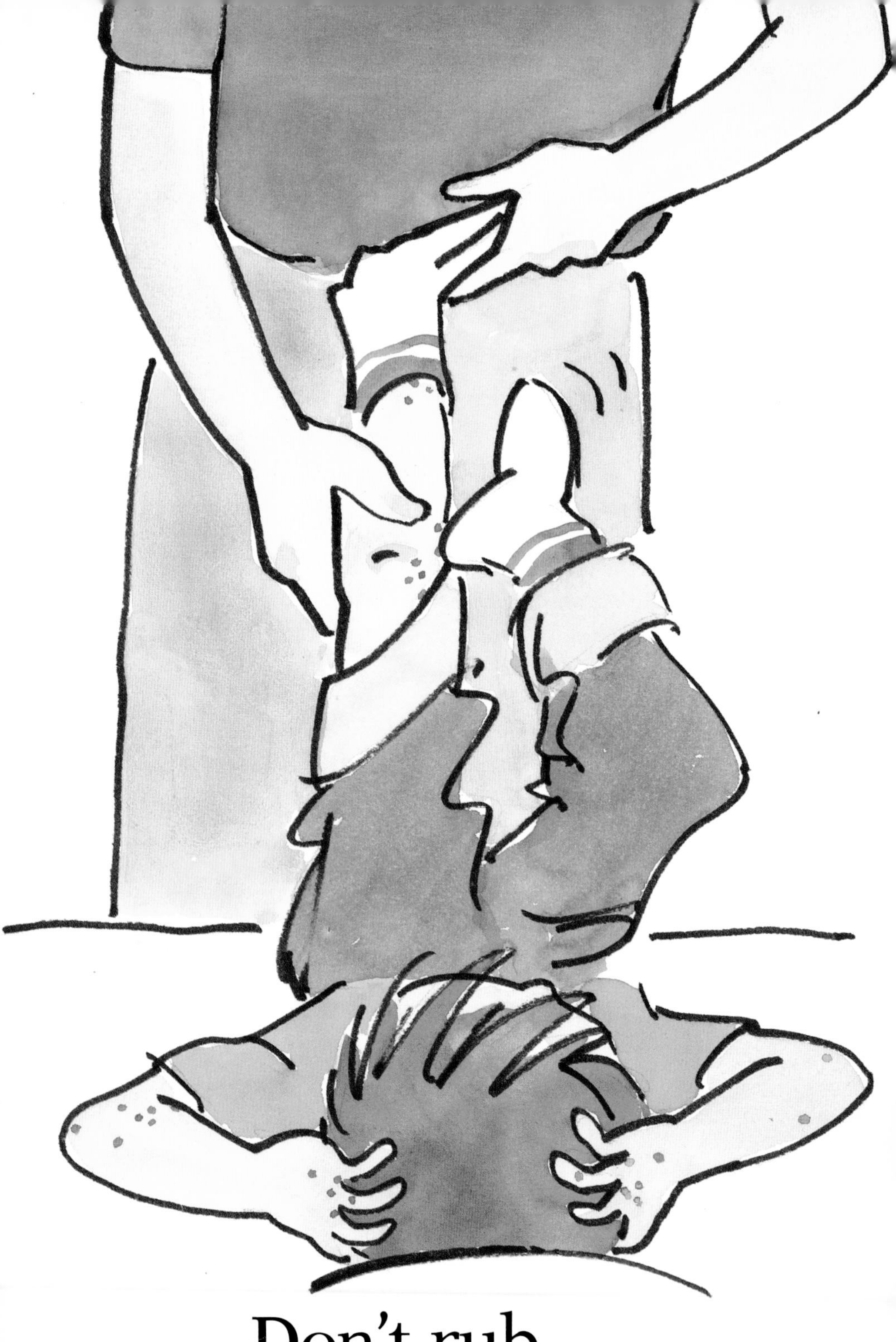

Don't rub.
Don't scratch.

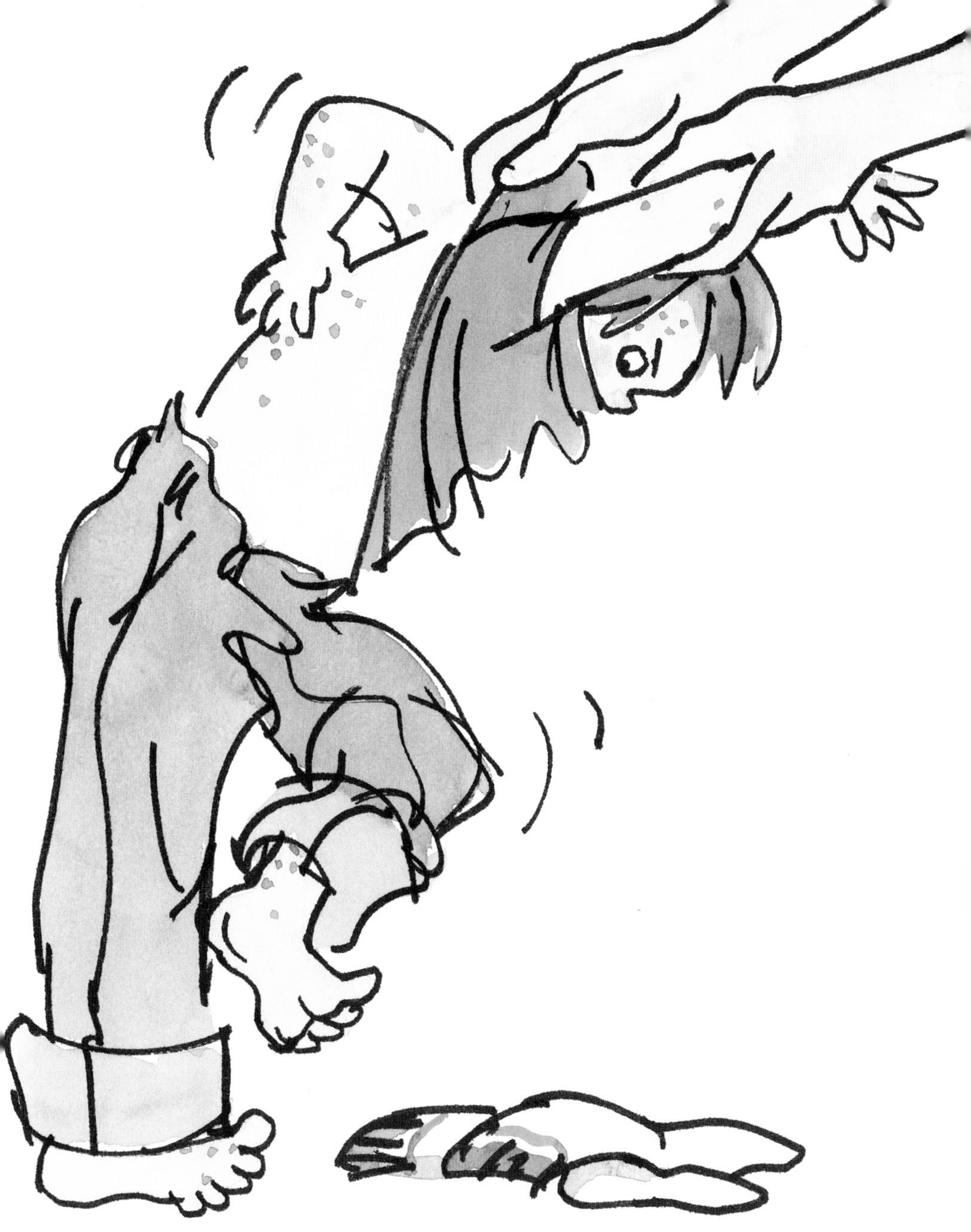

Oh, no!
Another batch!

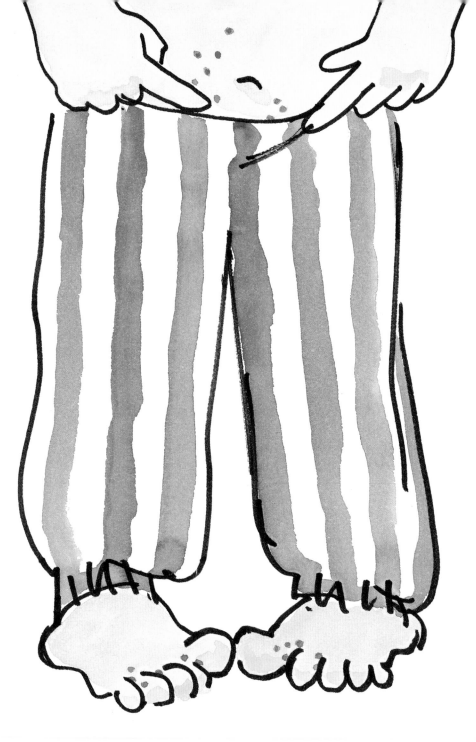

On my tummy,
between my toes,

down my back,
on my nose!

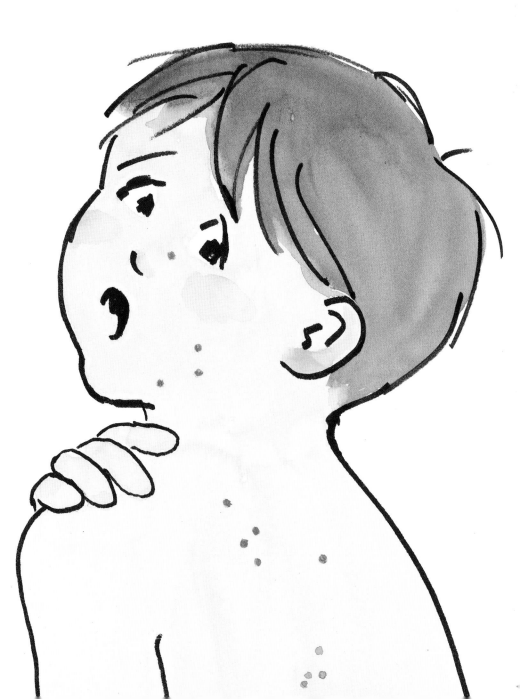

Lotion on.
Itching's gone
just for now.

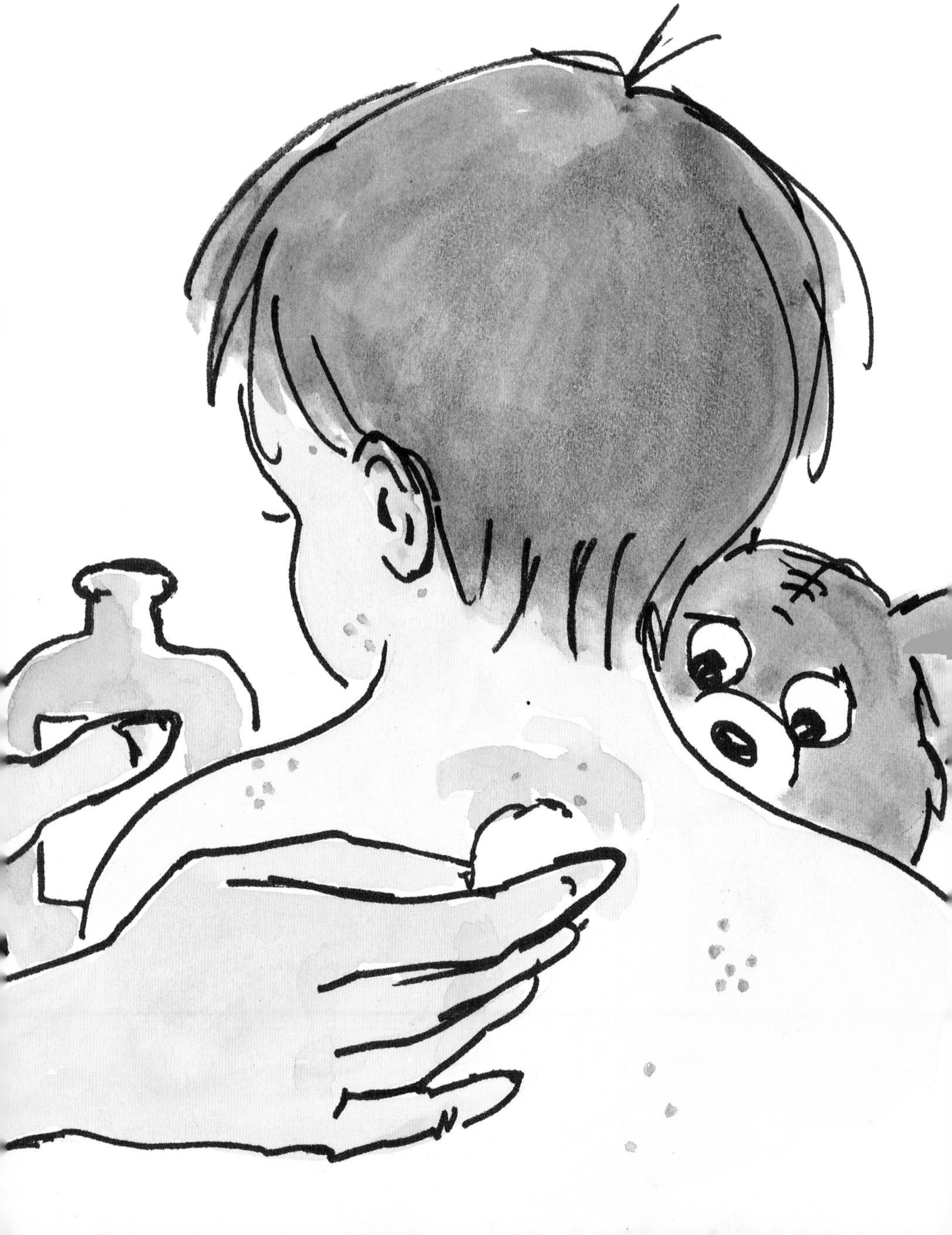

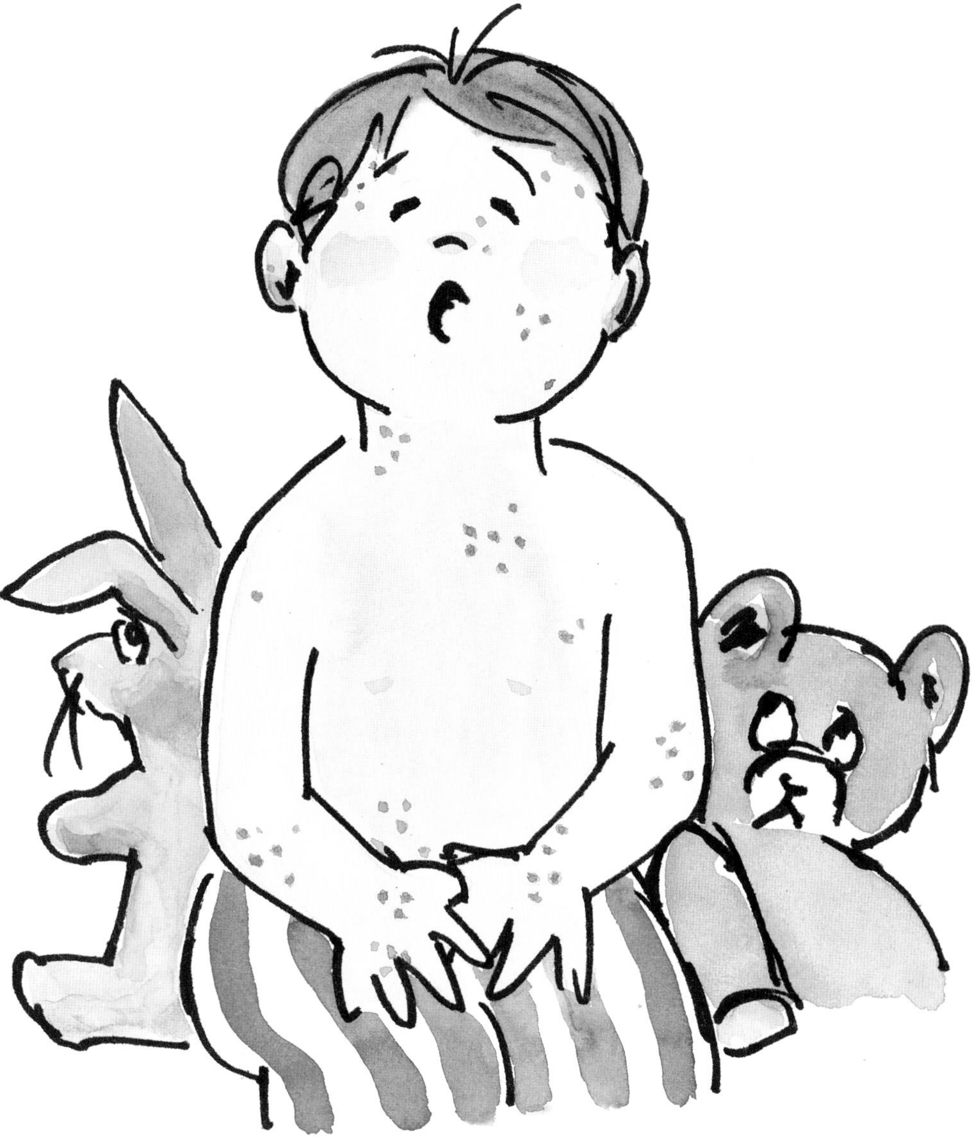

It comes back—
OW!

One and two
and three and four.
Five and six…
and more and more.

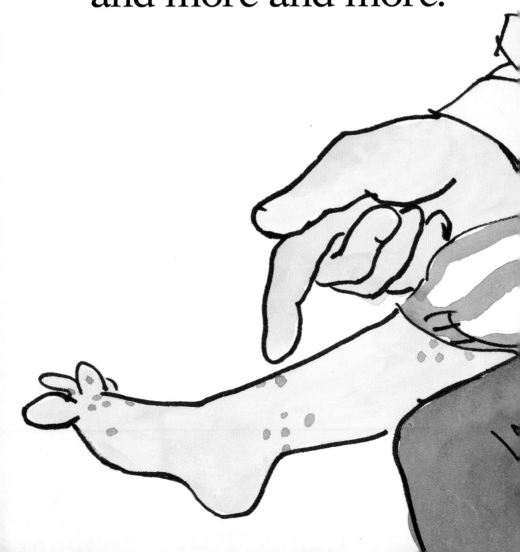

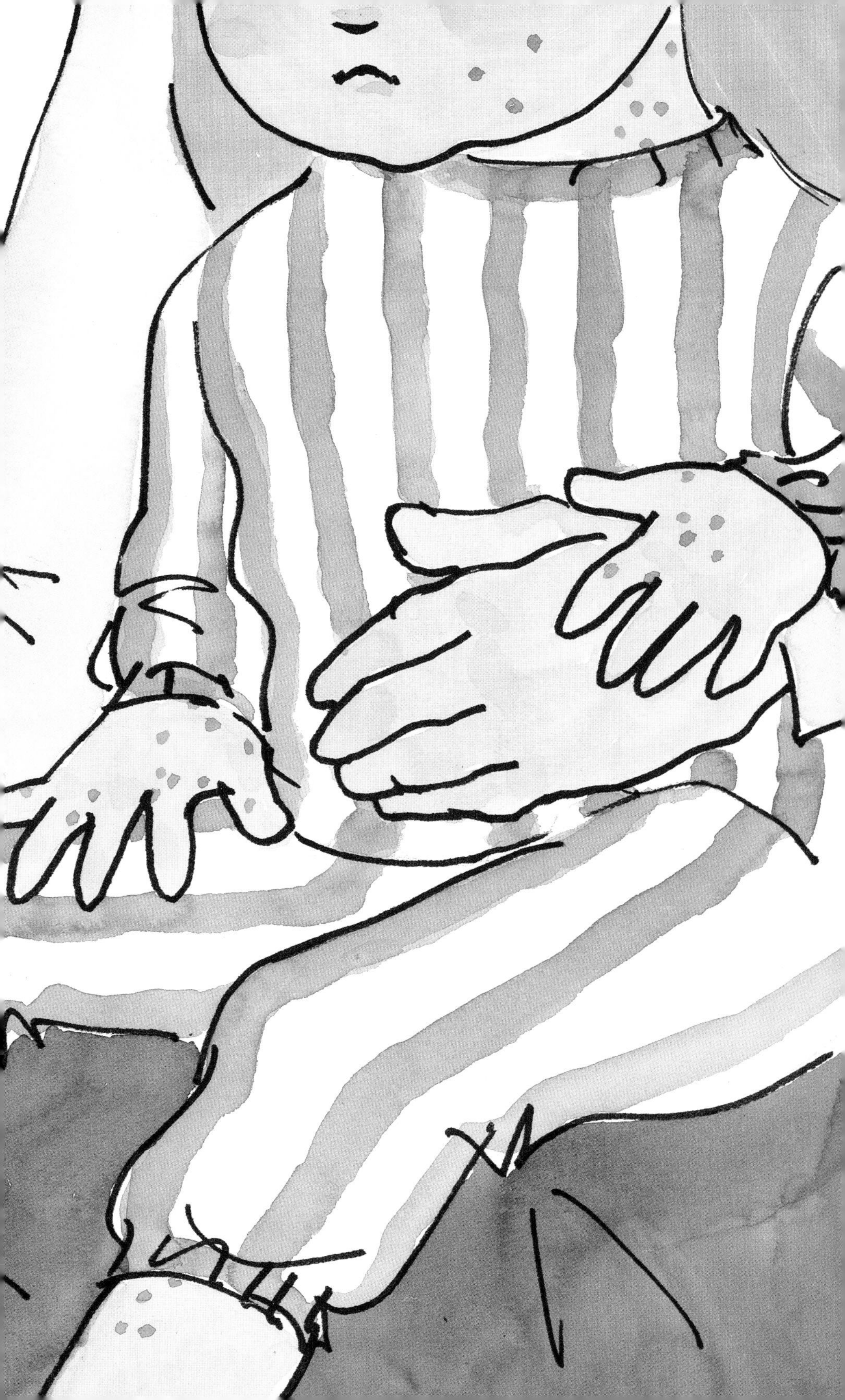

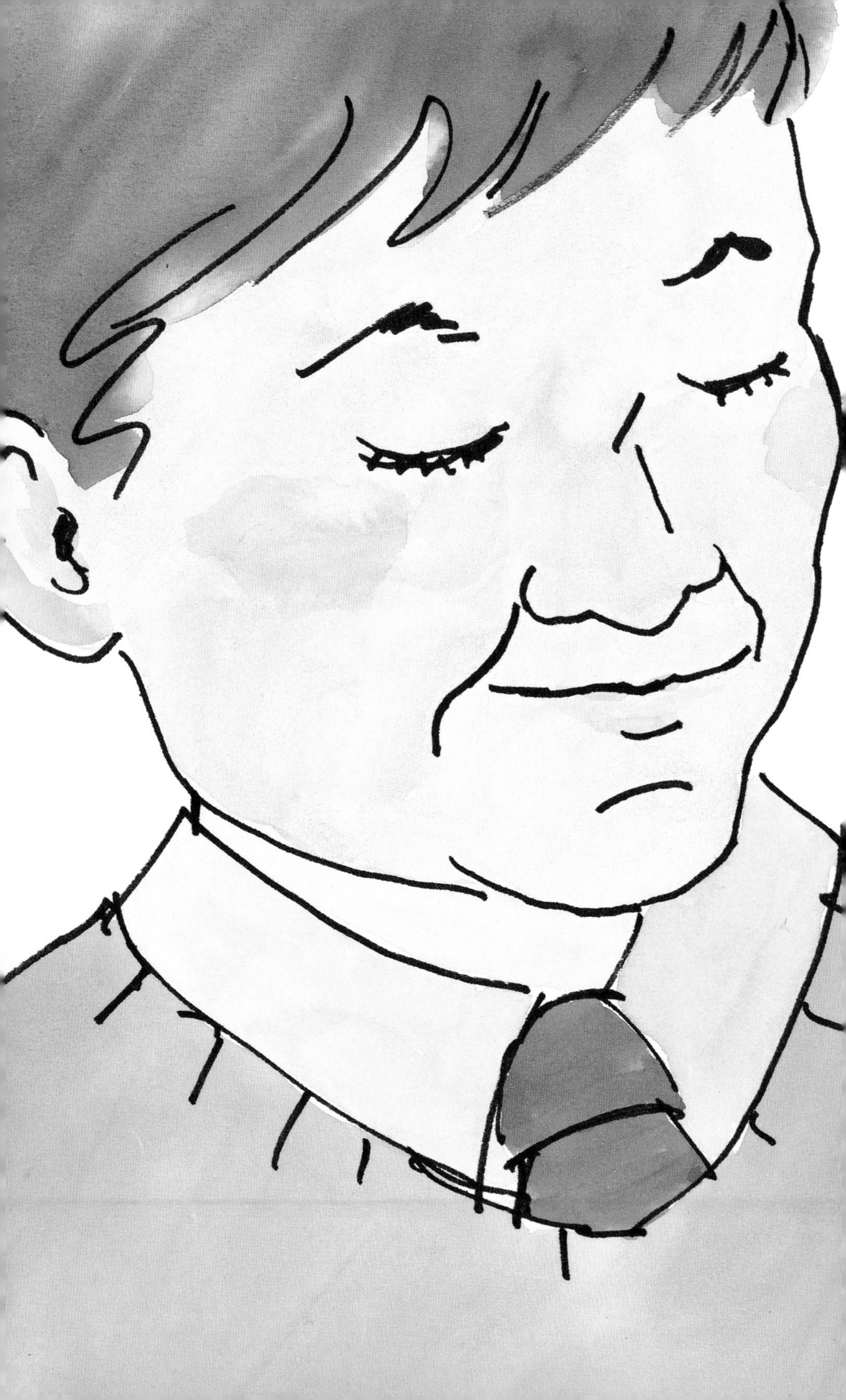

Daddy counts
my itchy spots.
Lots and lots
of chicken pox.

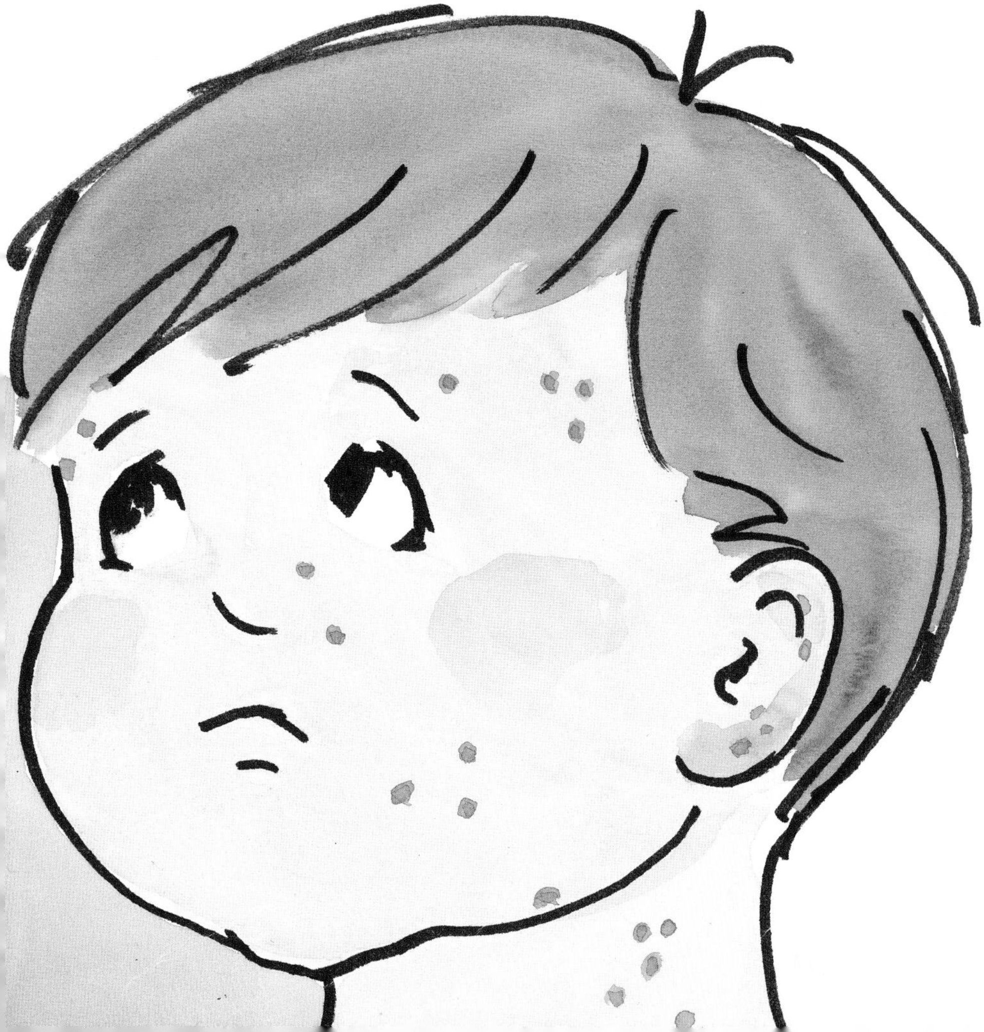

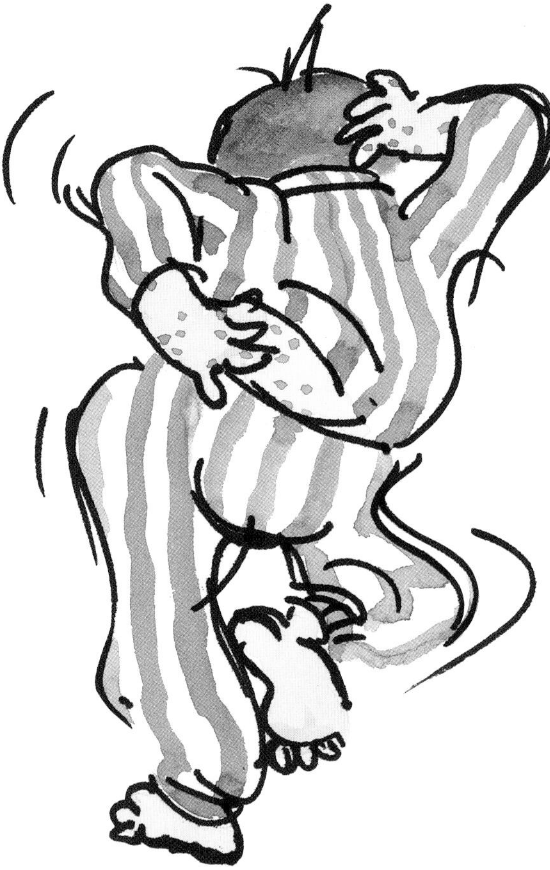

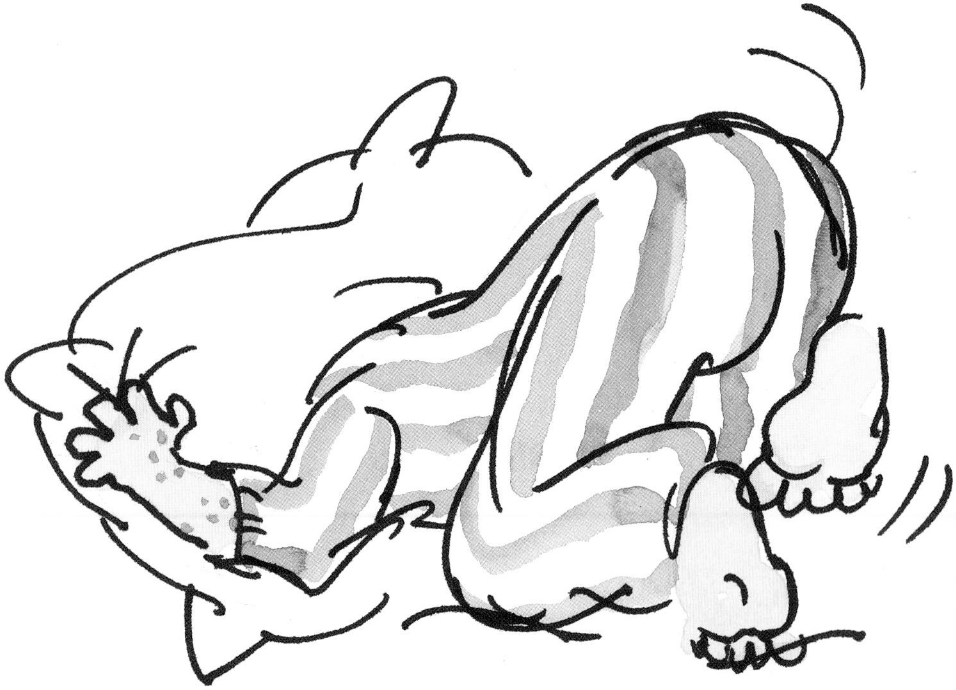

Itchy, itchy,
I feel twitchy....

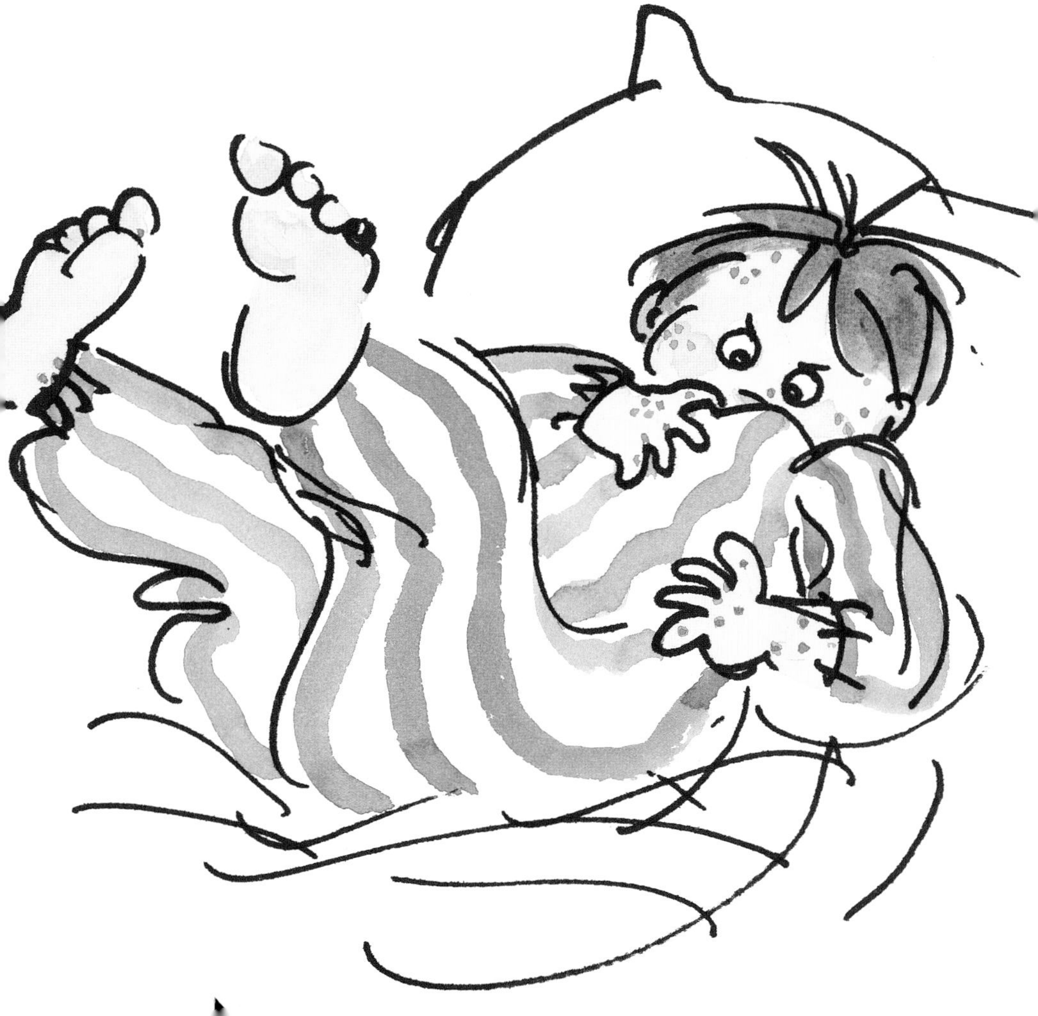

I run away.
The itching stays.

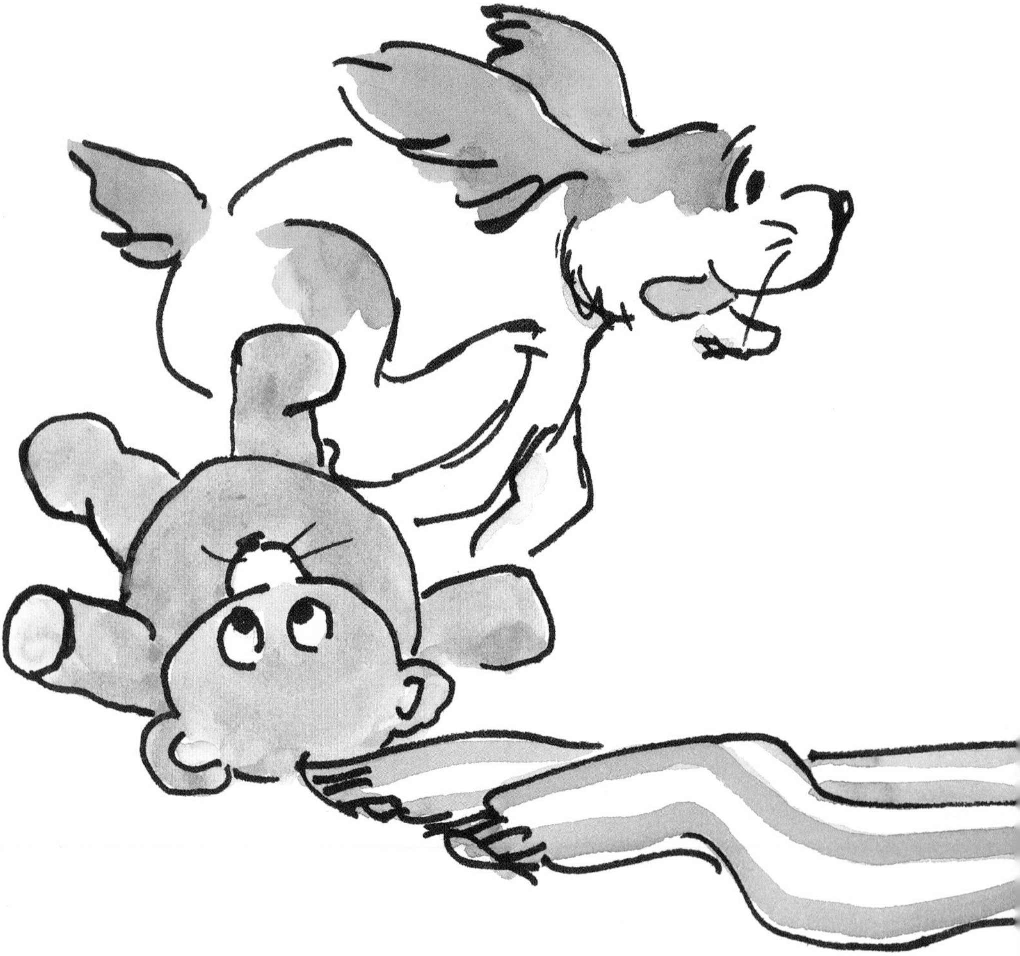

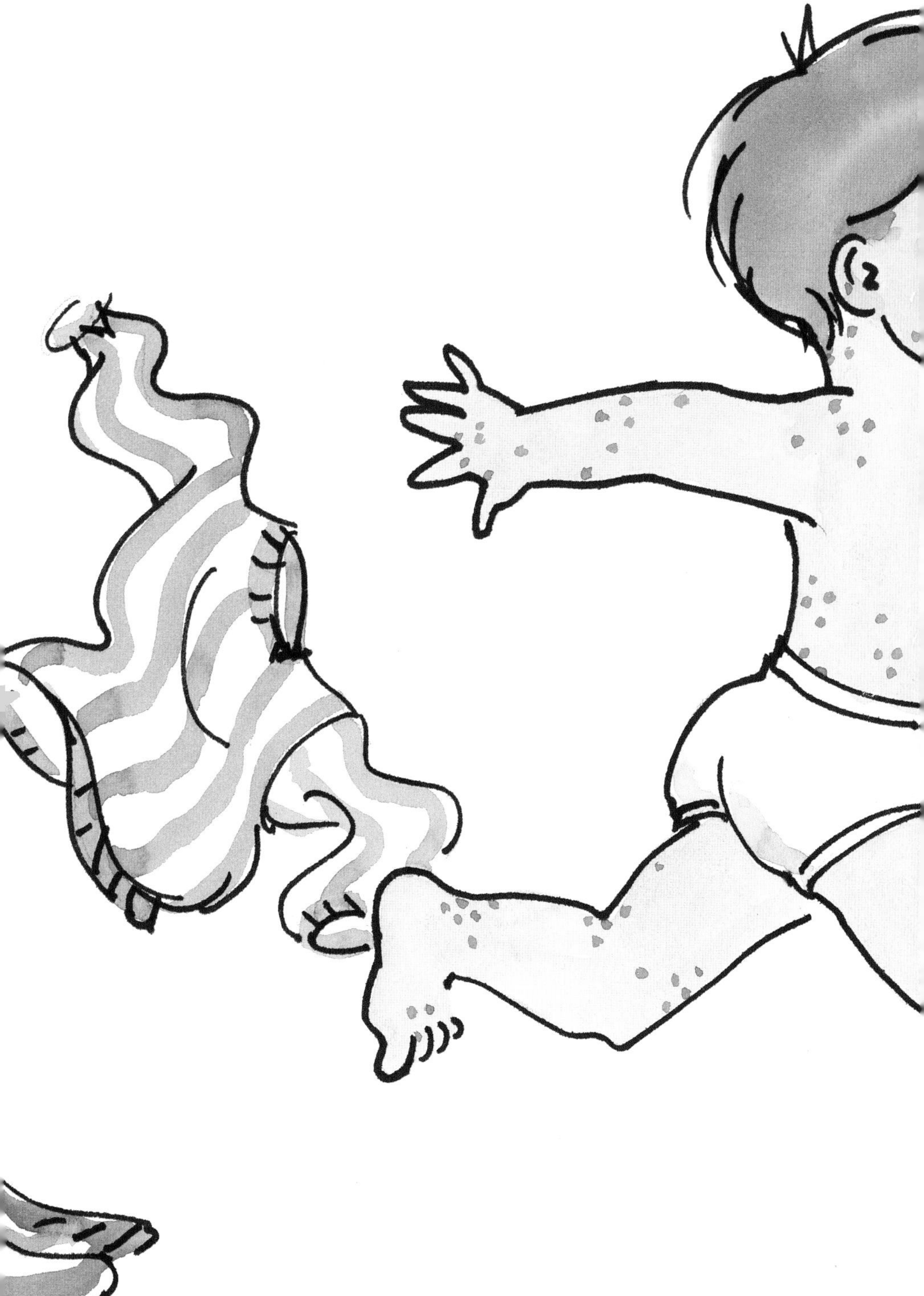

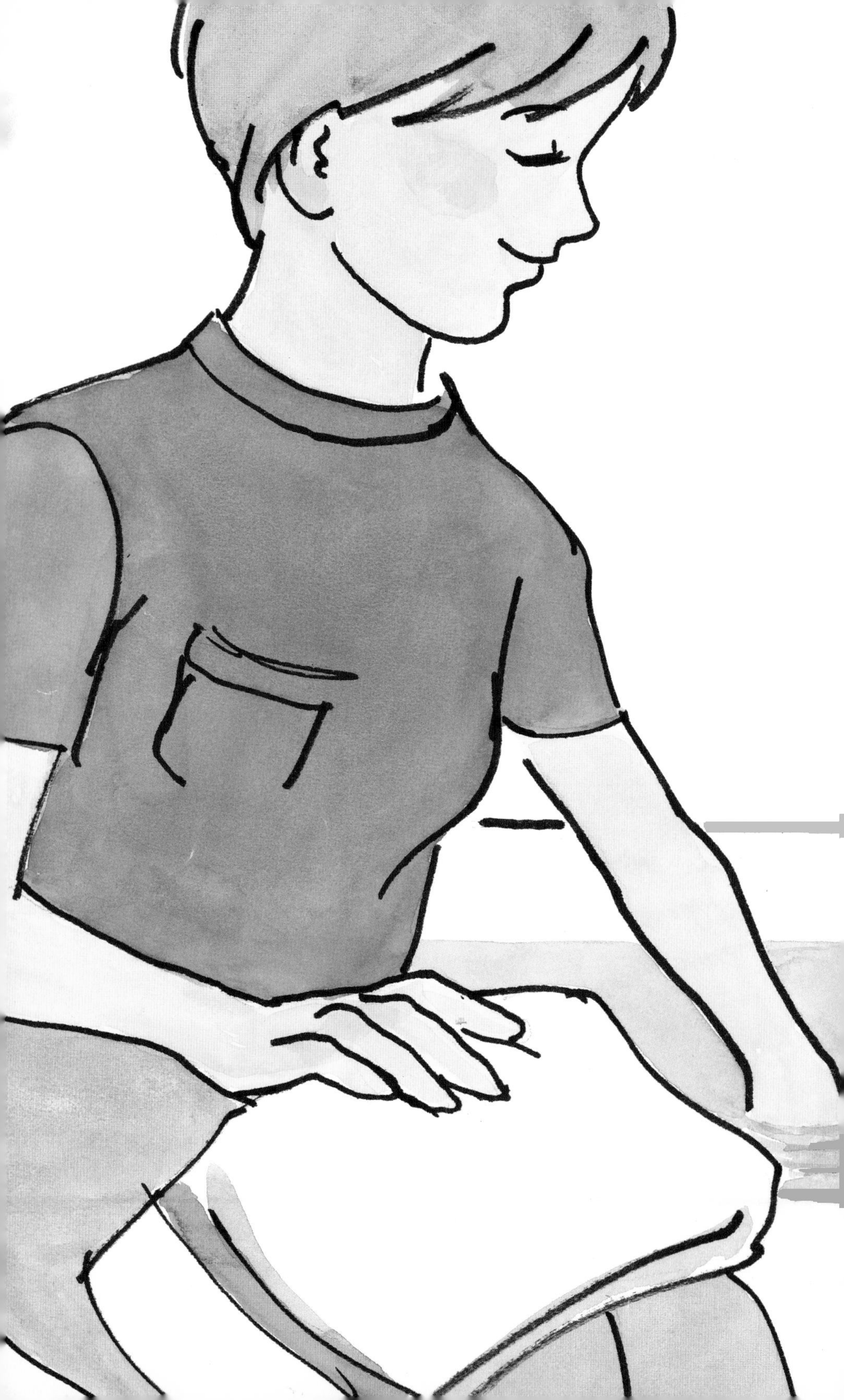

Rubber ducky doesn't
like my yucky, mucky
oatmeal bath.
But Mommy says
it's good for me.

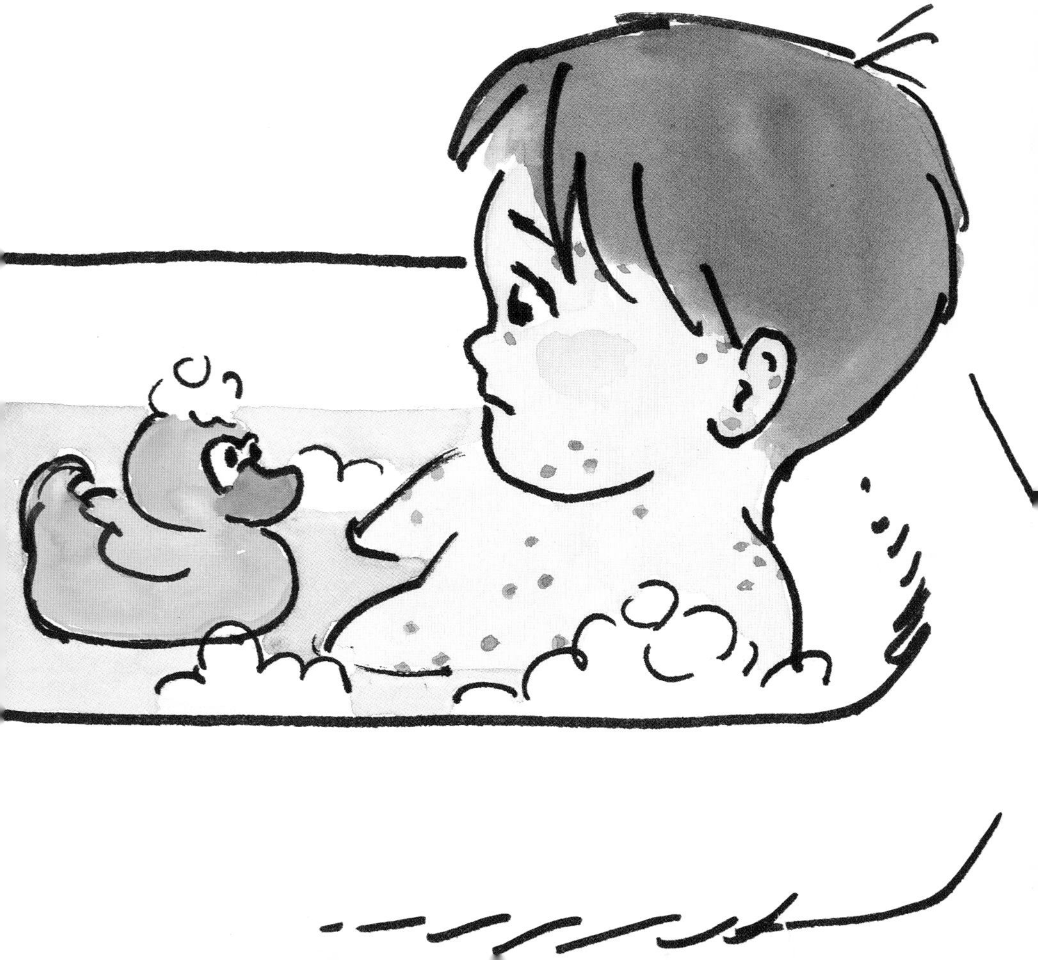

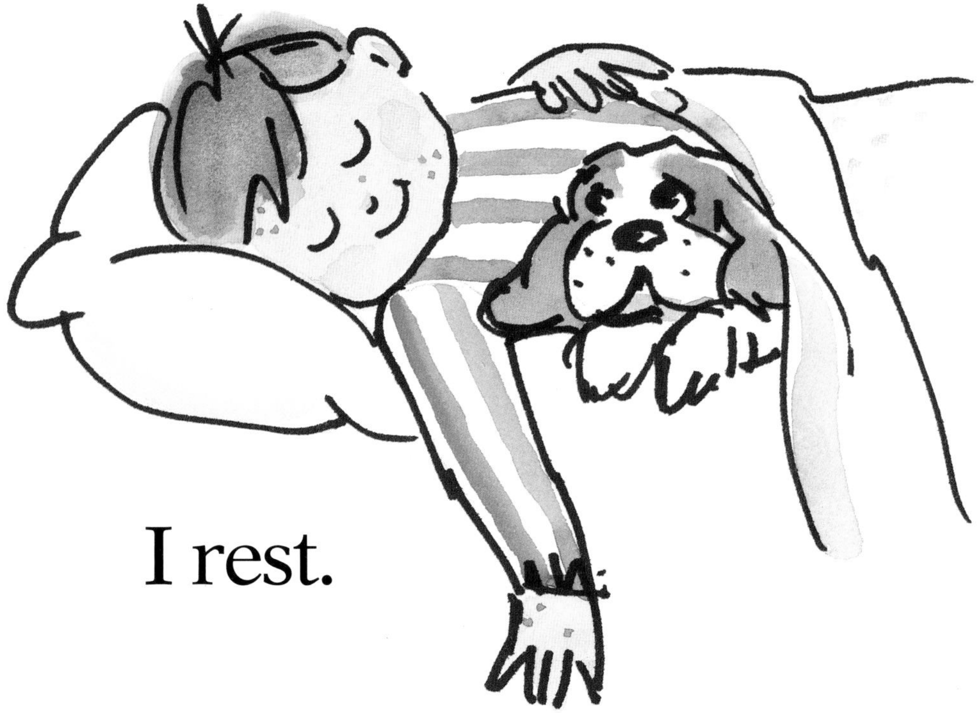

I rest.

I read.

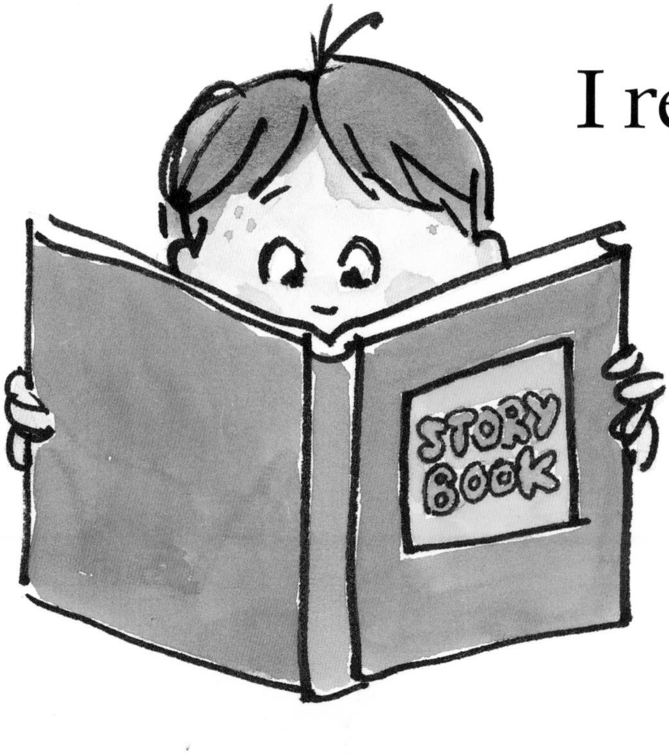
STORY
BOOK

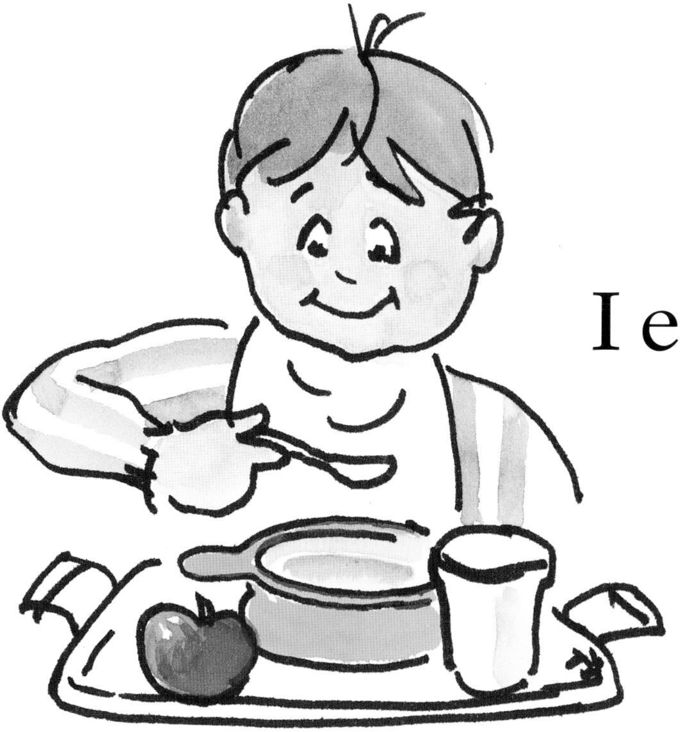

I eat.

I play.

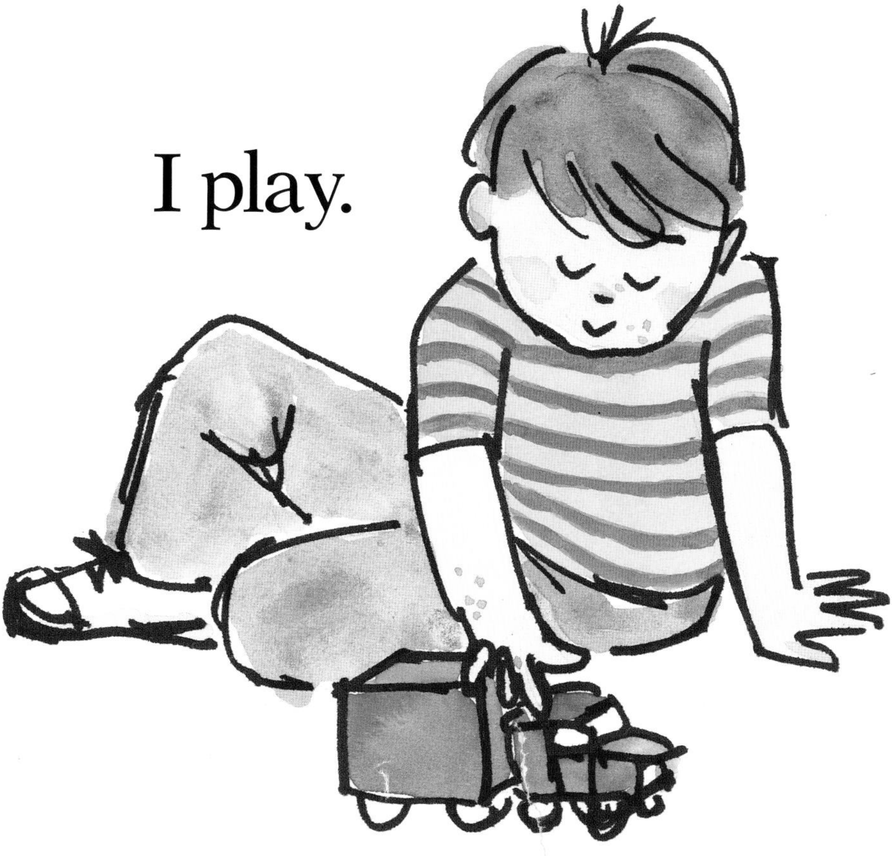

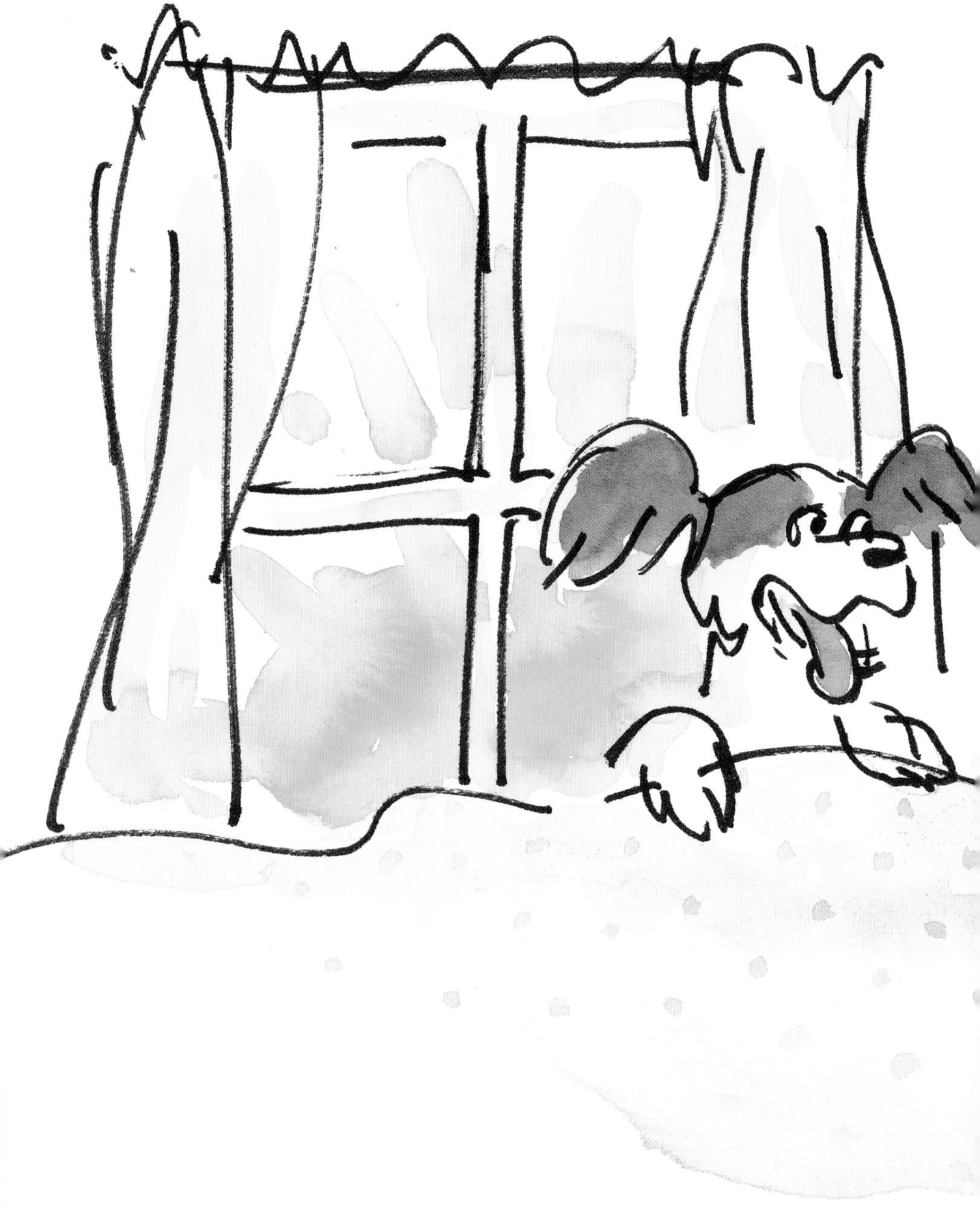

I feel better
every day.

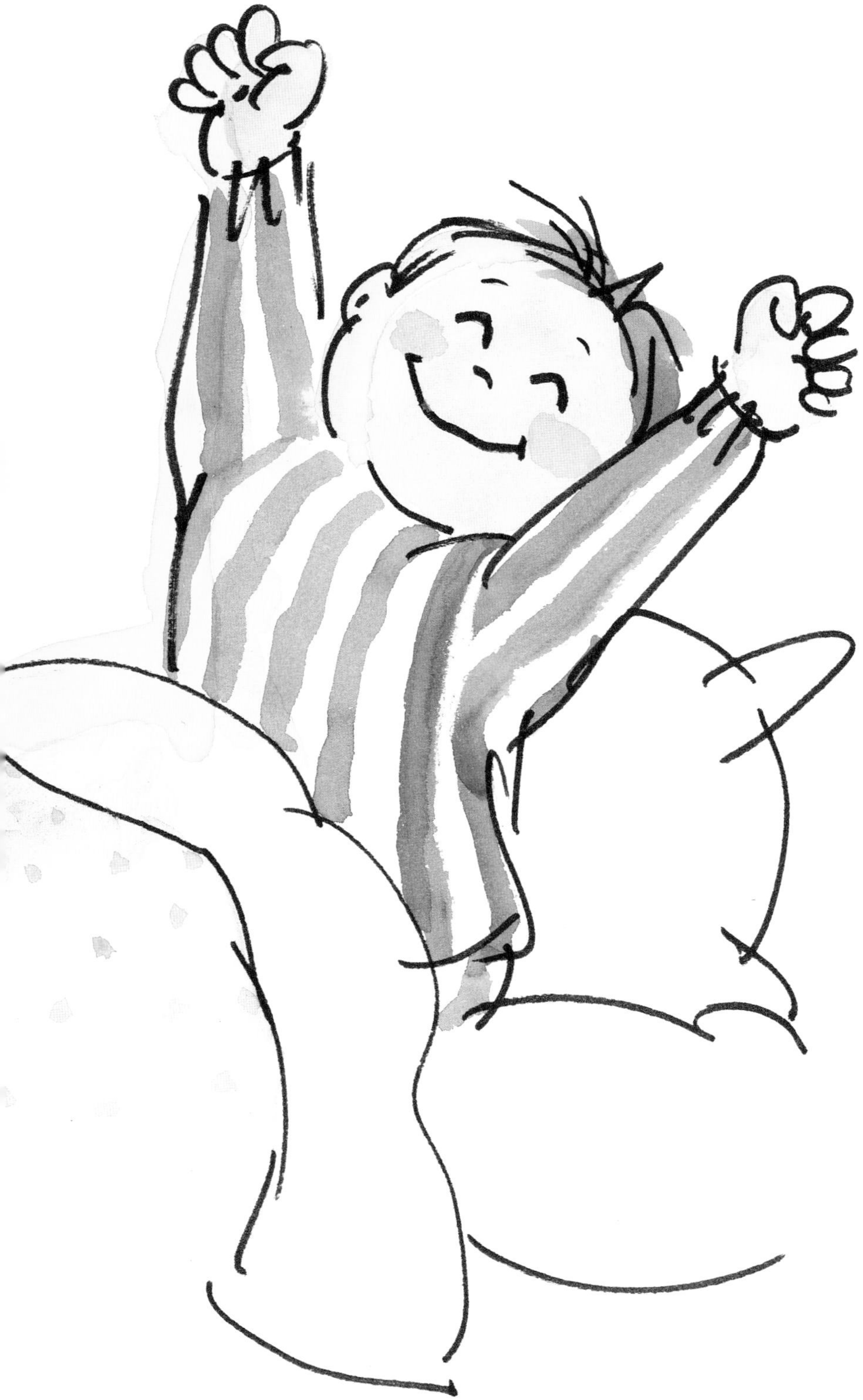

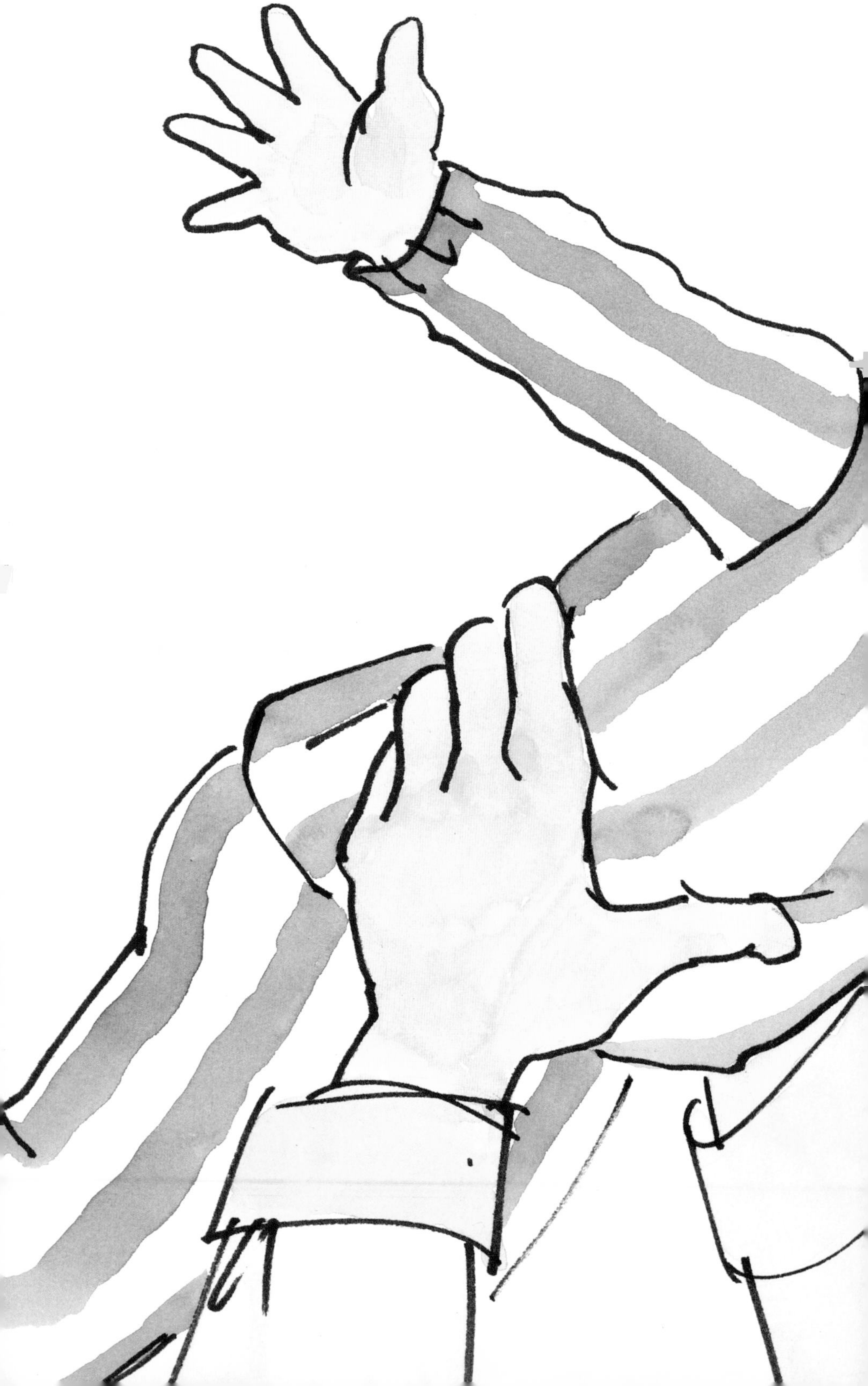

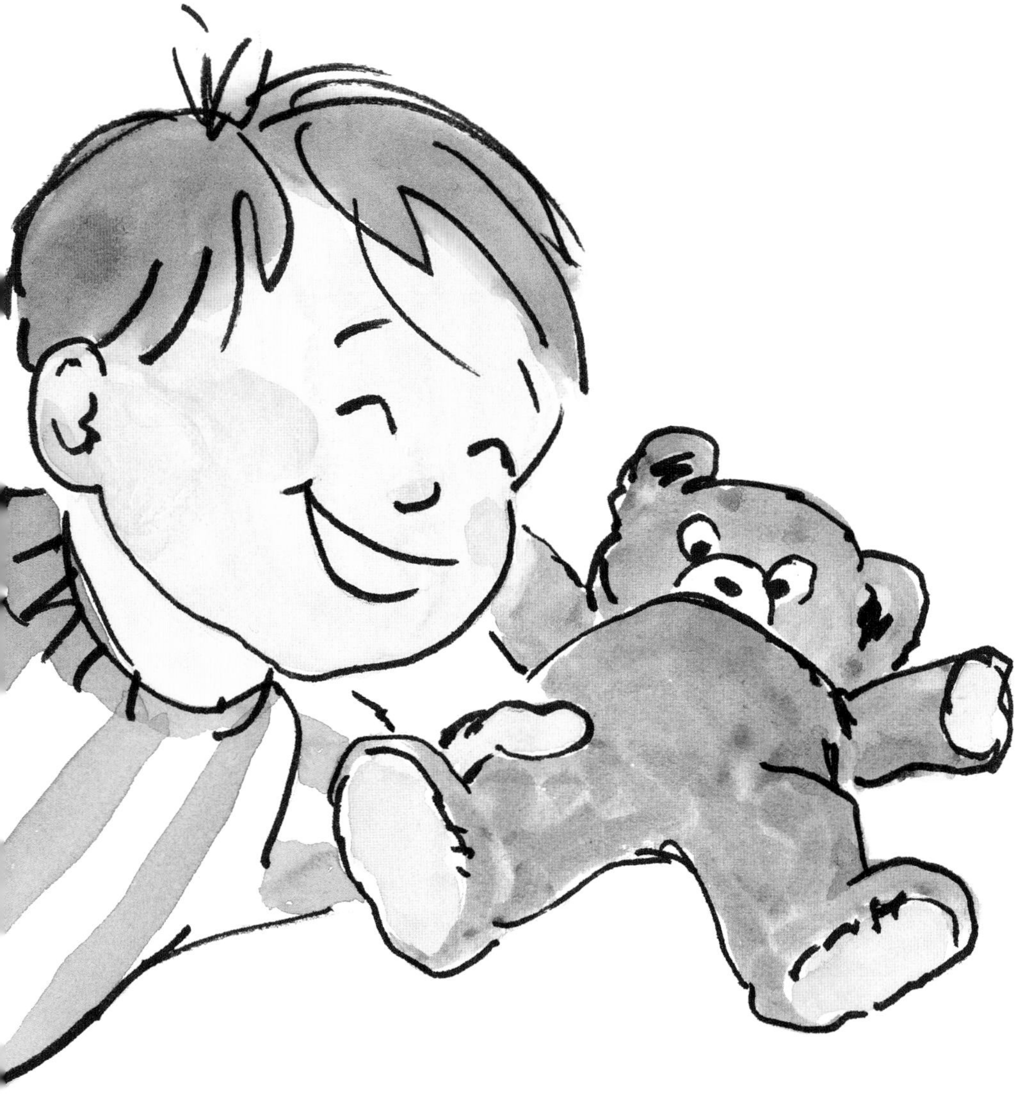

And then...
no new spots.
Hooray!

I'm okay!
I get to go
to school today!

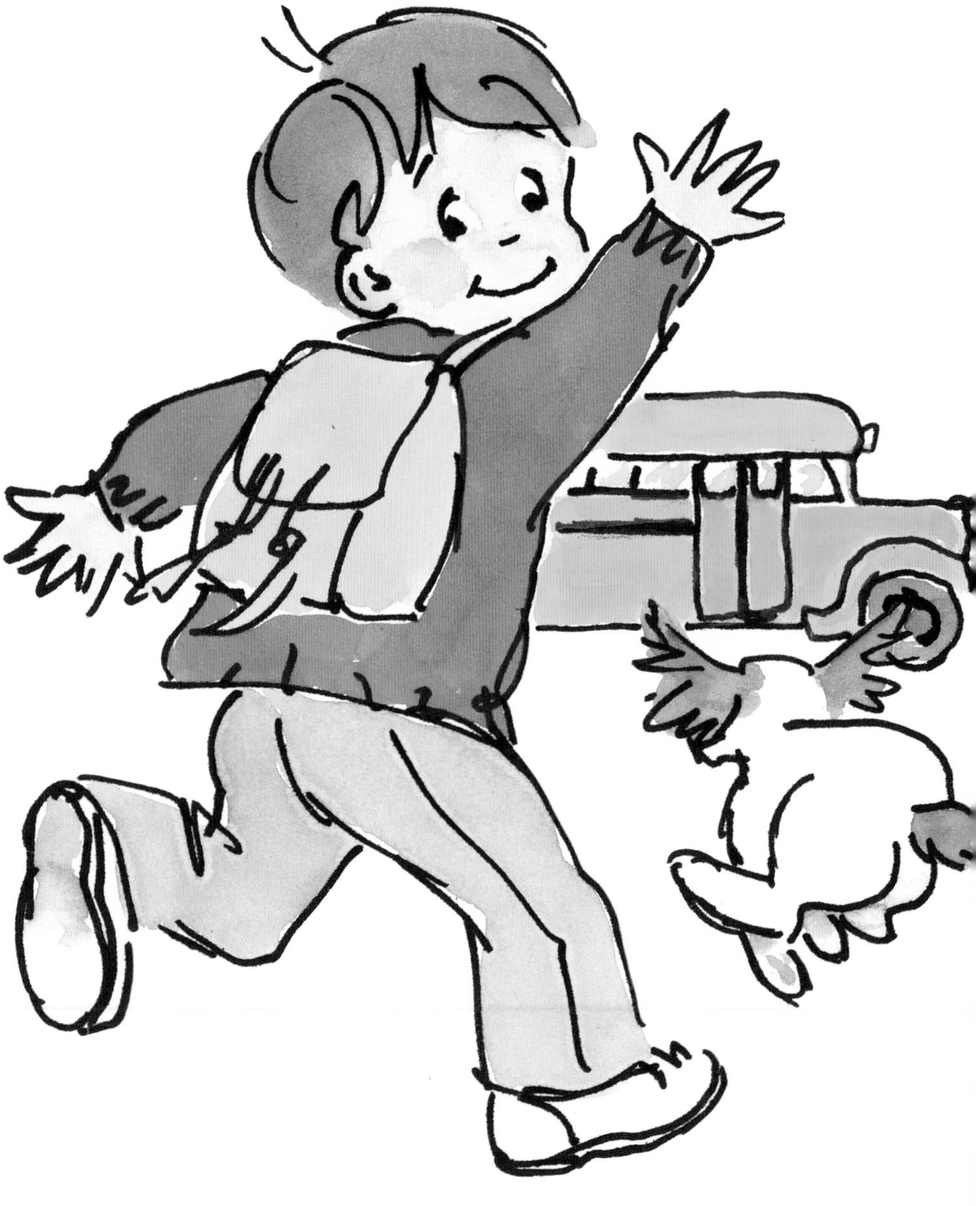